Changing Lanes with God as My CEO

CHANGING LANES

with

GOD AS MY CEO

By: Tawisha Nikki Buckingham

ISBN: 979-8-9929721-8-4 (Paperback)
Library of Congress Control Number (LCCN): 2025924755

Published by Remnant Media Publications

Printed in the United States of America

Dedication

I dedicate this book to my family, my legacy. My children, VP Jr. (my first heartbeat and my guardian angel) and VV (my second heartbeat and my young queen), have been the source of my strength and determination in life. As God's precious gifts to me, I have led them in the way God has guided me, with love, stability, faith, and encouragement. They have learned to place God at the center of their lives and to trust Him in all circumstances.

To my son, VP Jr:

As a baby boy, you brought the best out of me as I pressed forward with everything in me to prepare the best life for you, and in whatever challenge I had to face to do it. With you in my life, giving up was not an option. My soul misses you every day. I know that you are with me in spirit, and so my goal is always to make you proud. I love you more than words can say.

To VV, my young queen:

God already knew that we would need each other even more after losing VP Jr. Our bond and my love for you are timeless. I know that my prayers for you and my grandbabies are being received by God because

I see the strength and love that you exude each day as you mother them. I thank God for carrying us each day as we navigate this life without our angel. I am so thankful that VP Jr.'s spirit shows us his presence often, and so we hold every encounter very close to our hearts and will continue to do so until we see him again. Thank you for being an amazing daughter, sister, and mother.

"Changing Lanes with God as my CEO: Finding Purpose and Prosperity through Divine Direction" is the vehicle that I am using to thank God for carrying me through every difficulty that I have faced. I did not prevail by my own strength but by His grace, mercy, and special gift of resilience.

Through the quiet times of isolation during life's obstacles, I have learned my purpose, and I have claimed peace, joy, and favor in my walk with God. I not only dedicate this book to Him who has called me to write and speak in truth, love, and power, but I will continue to dedicate my life to Him. He is my light, strength, peace, and my everything. I thank Him for His goodness then, His goodness now, and His goodness that is to come.

"Blessed shall you be when you come in,
and blessed shall you be when you go out."

\- Deuteronomy 28:6-8

Acknowledgments

"Give to everyone what you owe them…

if respect, then respect; if honor, then honor."

- Romans 13:7

I give full honor, praise, and acknowledgment to my Father, God in Heaven, who has been my source in everything that I aspire to do or have been called by Him to do. I pray all things in His matchless, holy name. His guidance, love, and covering never fail. Lord, there is no other like you.

I would like to acknowledge my parents, Shirley, Bobby, and Tony and my grandparents, Otis Sr., Lucille, James Sr., Lura Mae, Joseph, and Gladys, as they were the vessels that God used to create my existence here on earth, they introduced me to God and have poured into me what I needed to sustain, grow and build in life. Their love and the prayers that they have spoken over me as a child are still covering me today.

I acknowledge my children, VP Jr., VV, and my grandchildren, Jolani—our family's tricuspid atresia heart warrior and God's Babygirl. We are all so very proud of her for the fight in her —Josiah, Jurzi, and Jireh, for their existence, which gives me the reason to walk in diligence and to remain committed to my goals and efforts in life. My love for them is deeply rooted in this mindset.

I acknowledge my Aunt T and my Uncle Paul (may your soul rest in holy peace, Uncle) for stepping to the plate when I needed a team and village for my new baby boy while I was away at college finishing key coursework that was required of me to complete my bachelor's degree. I can't express enough gratitude and thankfulness to you for having my back in this very important time and milestone in my life. I will forever appreciate you!

I acknowledge my spiritual counselor and friend, Ms. Violet S., who has been a driving force in praying over me and in encouraging me to remain focused on God's plan when I faced the biggest transition in my career and the struggles that I was encountering at that same time in my life. Her words of wisdom, deep understanding of Scripture, and accountability breathed a newness in my spirit. I thank God for sending Ms. Violet S. when I needed her the most. I wish that we had crossed paths sooner.

I acknowledge close family and friends, new and old (you know who you are), who have been there for me in prayer, wisdom, encouragement, purposeful conversations, invitations to meaningful fellowship opportunities, and by interceding in ways that guided me as I positioned myself to experience and receive God's very best in my life. The blessings through these spiritual and divine connections will continue to carry me through my next chapter in life and in the next assignment spoken to me by God. This type of preparedness begins with a willing spirit, assigned destiny helpers with genuine souls, and by embracing and walking in the unwavering purpose that is sent directly from my Father, God.

Table of Contents

Preface:

Trusting God Beyond the Plan

I once believed that success in life came from having a solid plan, setting goals, following the rules, and staying the course. I believed that if I worked hard, made responsible decisions, and remained faithful, life would unfold neatly and predictably. What I learned instead is that God often works far beyond our plans, and His purpose is revealed most clearly when we are willing to trust Him through uncertainty.

"Changing Lanes with God as My CEO" is a reflection of the seasons in my life when the road ahead was unclear, the timing did not make sense, and the responsibility felt heavier than I could carry on my own. These were the moments when I had to decide whether I would cling to my own understanding or fully surrender to God's direction. Repeatedly, God proved that His leadership was not only necessary but also perfect.

This book is not a story of flawless faith or perfect decisions. It is a testimony of growth, resilience, and learning to follow God even when the path ahead looked nothing like what I had envisioned. Through motherhood, education, relationships, and unexpected challenges, God consistently showed Himself as Provider, Protector, and Guide, faithfully orchestrating each step of my journey.

I hope that as you read these pages, you will be encouraged to trust God beyond your plans. Whether you are standing at a crossroads, navigating a difficult transition, or learning how to release control, this book serves as a reminder that God's plans are always higher, wiser, and rooted in purpose.

When we allow Him to lead, every detour becomes meaningful, and every change of direction brings us closer to who He created us to be.

CHAPTER

One

How My Journey Began

God's protection over my life was very clear early on as I grew as a small fetus in my mother's womb. At six months of gestation with me, my mother and I were directly confronted by danger from someone with horrific plans to take us both out through a forced miscarriage. We would not have stood a chance in such a vulnerable state, which would be unimaginable to anyone. In the most critical time in our lives, God's protective hand covered both of us in that hour, and He continues to lead and guard our lives with His love, protection, and guidance today. I thank my Father, Abba, for life, for a mother who is steadfast and immovable, and for the opportunity to share with the world the grace and mercy that God has bestowed on me and my family time and time again.

I was born in Upstate New York, to teenage parents, Shirley and Bobby, in the 70s. I am my mother's first child of five and my father's second child of six. Some time later, my mother and my stepfather, Tony, created a blended family in which we inherited bonus brothers and sisters, and great family memories were created over the years. So, I come from a rather large family that consists of lots of siblings, and it continues to swiftly grow today with grandchildren and great-grandchildren. Family is a blessing, and we had grown as children to value the family unit and foundation and to always stick together in love and support.

My mother named me *"Tawisha,"* and most of my life, I have been asked what my name means. As a child, whenever I asked my mother the meaning of my name, she would tell me that her sister, my Aunt T, told her to give me this name because she dreamed of my mom naming me *"Tawisha"* when she learned that my mother was pregnant with me. For several years, I was asked by several people about the meaning of my name, and so I always shared with them the same story. For quite some time, I was always told that it was a beautiful name, and so I simply held onto that factor and that factor alone. I had never thought to look deeper into the meaning of the name, Tawisha.

Later in life, when I was in my early 30s, one of our senior managers at the company where I worked, UF, asked me the meaning of my name on different occasions. I responded to him with the same answer every time, telling him of the dream that my aunt had. I now believe that he was giving me the cue to take the initiative to research the meaning of my name. Unbeknownst to me, after some time, he had taken the initiative himself and completed the research on my behalf.

One day, he asked me to stop by his office, and he told me of his research on the meaning and background of my name. He told me that my name comes from a city named *"Al Tawisha"* in the African country of Sudan. I was very surprised because I literally thought that my birth-given name was just a name that crossed my aunt's mind while she was asleep one day. I never thought to look any further than accepting that fact. I now know and understand that the name *"Tawisha"* was spoken to my aunt and was communicated directly to her by the voice of God as she slept. I was so grateful for his efforts and determination in helping me to discover such a deep and inspirational connection to the root of my being. I thank God for such a transformative encounter! This revelation gave me a new grounding and footing on the path where God has placed me.

Having a strong sense of identity in who we are and in who God created us to be allows us to fulfill our purpose in the life He gifted us and to do it with confidence, authenticity, and great impact.

I also thank God for allowing me to cross paths with individuals who add groundbreaking substance and spirit-led purpose to my life. A stronger sense of pride and empowerment touched my entire being and the trajectory of my life journey when I learned about the origin of my name. I gained a reinforced sense of self-reflection, self-respect, and self-honor that I still carry within my spirit and soul.

Sudan is a country located in northeastern Africa that has an ancient past of turmoil and civil war crisis (the country is still experiencing the crisis in the present day). It's a country of rich culture, profound ancient history, and great struggles, but still resilient with deep hope for its people and its future. The name Sudan is derived from the Arabic expression, bilad-al-sudan, meaning *"Land of the Blacks,"* a term used by Arabic geographers to describe the regions south of the Sahara Desert where African populations lived.

Islam and the Arabic language became dominant across much of northern Sudan, while indigenous African languages and cultures remained stronger in the south. Before its 2011 separation from South Sudan, Sudan made up over eight percent of the African continent. Its capital, Khartoum, lies near the continent's center, often called the *"heart"* of Africa, at the meeting point of the Blue Nile and White Nile rivers. This area is one of Africa's largest urban centers and a major hub for commerce, attracting both public and private enterprise.

Sudan is also the homeland of the Kingdom of Kush, an ancient Nubian civilization known for its many pyramids and its rich blend of Nubian and Egyptian influence. It has a diversity of ethnic groups and is the land where the Nile River flows directly down its middle, providing richness to its land, allowing its people to conveniently thrive from the fruitfulness of its soil.

The connection that I feel with the country of Sudan is very much deep in spirit, heartfelt in culture, and compassionate in how it strives to restore peace and unity within its borders and beyond through the power and spirit of resilience. This connection of resilience allows me to embrace a stronger sense of who I am and what I have been placed on this earth to fulfill with the guidance and direction of God.

The relationship that we have with the Almighty God begins with birth and the name that we are to bear as we walk our designated journeys. Our names are announced before we are introduced to and before we interact with others. So with this life-changing revelation, I now have a powerful sense of understanding, purpose, and alignment with the name that God has chosen for me through direct encounters and experiences that my journey continues to unveil to me. Because of this confirmation and clarity, I now walk in full self-awareness of who I am, a daughter of the King, the Most High God, born to walk in the confidence of resilience, which will always be my greatest strength and superpower no matter what life throws my way.

The responsibilities that I was given as a big sister helped to groom me into the woman and mother that I am today. The responsibilities of being the oldest child built up something in me that grade school or college could never do. This process grew with me over time, requiring a strong sense of accountability and patience. I was proud of being a big sister, and I took this role seriously, although my younger siblings got on my nerves at times (lol, this is usually what younger siblings do, right? Am I the only one who feels this way?). I enjoyed assisting my mom with chores most of the time, and I helped to keep things in order around the house. In the meantime, my mom would allow me to pick out something *"cute"* at the mall whenever the opportunity allowed, as a treat for my assistance, creating a mini monster when it came to the love of fashion and the mindset of working hard to acquire nice things of my liking.

As the big sister who was helpful around the house, my mother and stepfather would make a special stop for me at the nearest mall, where we stayed overnight while traveling on vacation to whatever town we were en route to visit. Those road trips were the best, and they carry great family memories and great anticipation every summer.

The role that I inherited as a big sister instilled in me a strong sense of character, dignity, confidence, and leadership. I always strived to put my best foot forward because my younger siblings were watching. My influence on them mattered to me. Older siblings set the tone of the energy for the children in the household most of the time, and they quietly set the radar for the younger siblings, in my honest opinion. There are times when a younger sibling tries to test an older sibling, seeing how far they can go before the older sibling gives a reaction or is forced to remind the younger sibling who they are to them. An example of this is when I was in high school, I caught my younger sister wearing an outfit of mine to school. Since I left for school earlier than her, she decided to go into my closet and pick out an outfit.

Did I mention that I don't like sharing my clothes? Did I mention how I knew exactly how my clothes and shoes were organized before leaving the house every day?

The situation went to the far left rather quickly when I made it back home that day before she did. Mom ended up assuming the role of referee by default, breaking us apart like rams that locked horns.

As a high school student, I was very territorial about my clothes, shoes, and purses, and would consider possibly sharing with my siblings when asked, maybe. That was a tough decision, as I would think in my teenage mind. How many of us share this experience growing up? I know it was not just me who experienced this growing up in a house with siblings. Today, I would give my loved ones the shirt off my back if they needed it.

There is something powerful that develops in older siblings that brings value in being an example to their younger siblings, which later helps them to become strong leaders. In my childhood, like most children, playing outside was my favorite thing to do. From hide and seek to kickball to double-dutch, you name it, we did it. Mud pies, hide-and-seek, and riding our bikes across town, to the local parks, and back were a pastime for me, my cousins, and my neighborhood friends. We were children at a time when playing outdoors and riding our ten-speed Huffy bikes were the most fun. We also knew that when the streetlights popped on, it was time to head home on time if we wanted to experience the great outdoor fun again anytime soon. So, we knew not to risk it.

For indoor fun, we also learned from older cousins how to play Spades, Tunk, and Uno. These games were super fun until one of the younger cousins frivolously pulled out a playing card that caused us to lose the game. Suddenly, a thickness of frustration was in the air, and so we had to find something else to do for fun. They did us wrong, right?

The children of today seem to enjoy being consumed with indoor activities, with entertainment from cell phones, social media, computers, and video games. So, I feel that they are missing out on the beauty and splendor of God's creation in the great outdoors and nature. With that, I still believe in the importance of enrolling children in indoor and outdoor sports and activities that will develop in them a form of balance, structure, and well-roundedness inside and outside of the four walls of home and school. Yes, I am that type of mother. Trust me, they will thank us later.

The icing on the cake is the ability to bless our children with worldly cultural experiences and the opportunity to become well-travelled early in life, experiencing other countries and cultures, and building up an inner confidence in knowledge and open-mindedness in a world filled with many differences. These types of experiences help children to learn about the similarities and the differences of others outside of themselves, which will allow them to establish a sense of compassion for others, including those who live in other countries and cultures. This same outlook will be for those from countries and cultures who have chosen to visit or live in our country as well. This type of exposure will sustain them in any environment.

I often reflect on how, in my youth, my parents planned a vacation for us where we experienced the country of Canada, which was four hours away from us in Upstate New York. Enjoying Niagara Falls and its history, and Marineland Amusement park as children, and listening to the residents speak fluent French in Quebec, observing their way of dress, their culture, and their interaction with each other left a long-lasting and impactful experience on us.

Although when my children were young, I had not yet connected traveling out of the country with them in their childhood as an opportunity to take advantage of these benefits in this way. However, as a grandmother, it is now at the forefront of our vacation plans. With that, we shall all gain this life-evolving and life-enriching exposure and experience that creates in us a grounding and a connection to the world that God created for us to learn and to embrace with the gift of humanity, honor, respect, and love.

As we all know, these experiences are best felt while basking in the county's culture, history, food, and air, which can't be explained in a textbook or magazine. It must be felt in the flesh and in the spirit. The family bonding, memories, and legacy in this type of traveling are priceless. According to Essence Magazine (By Brooke Sabin and Nora Wallaya, April 20, 2021), Jessica Nabongo traveled to all 195 nations and became the first Black woman to have documented this feat. She visited every country on Earth. She learned to *"Travel with kindness, travel with positive energy and travel without fear,"* says Jessica Nabongo. So, when traveling abroad, we should embrace kindness, positive energy, and fearlessness as we yield to the blessings from God with such great opportunities, experiences, and connections that shape us and our family values with substance, honor, and respect. We have traveled as a family throughout the United States, but traveling abroad will expand our hearts, minds, and spirits on a broader scale, and it will connect us as a family where our abroad memories together, away from familiar ground, will carry us the distance in our lives. I aim for meaningful and priceless family experiences and traditions that may continue through every generation.

As a youth, I attended Syracuse City School District schools at all three levels, elementary, middle, and high school. Shout out to my alma mater, McKinley Brighton Elementary, Delaware Elementary, Cathedral Elementary, Levy Middle School, and William Nottingham High School (Go Bulldogs!). Throughout my educational experiences, I was quite shy and reserved, yet I had quite a few friends and associates who brought out the social part of me that gave me the comfort that I needed to maintain some balance in my young life. I also had a first cousin, GG, who is six months younger than me, and so it made the process easier in the early stages of our social life because we relied on each other to help navigate every type of character, including the *"bullies."*

We were each other's first best friends, and we had each other's backs no matter what. When disagreements with others arose, we both were down for each other. We were each other's *"ride or die."* He did not play when it concerned me, and I did not play when it concerned him. So, when I was in time-out, guess who else was in time-out? That's right, GG.

Back in the day, when I had to move from one apartment to the next with little notice, my cousin, GG, rounded up his crew to make it happen. So, whenever GG reached out to me for help, I was there. We grew up together, raised to be close, later became adults, and began to expand our own families over the years. My son is his godson, and one of his daughters is my goddaughter.

First cousins are like siblings, and that is how we were raised. That still stands today, even though we reside in two different states and are grandparents now. We were raised to always stick together! How many of you and your first cousins were raised like siblings and were taught to have each other's backs no matter what?

There is nothing like the first cousin bond, as it shares the same *"glue"* as the sibling connection. It can be powerful in ways that will strengthen the family structure, incorporating unconditional love and support, and a family legacy that will remain intact over the years, making the family reunions and family gatherings a win. A solid and strong family bond will maintain a family legacy that our ancestors will be proud of.

As a middle schooler, my bedroom walls were wallpapered with New Edition, LL Cool J, and Michael Jackson posters from Right On! and Word Up! magazines. I was a regular subscriber, and I most definitely did not play about my weekly BET (Black Entertainment Television) lineup of Video Soul, Rap City, Teen Summit, Hits from the Streets, and, some years later, 106 and Park. My very first concert was Fresh Fest, where

GG and I rocked out in our 80s forward outfits, ready to watch Salt 'N Peppa, Fat Boys, Run DMC, Kurtis Blow, Whodini, and the likes, do what they did best as they lit up the stage. I was so excited to be in the building watching my favorites perform front and center for us, LIVE. I never wanted the show to end.

Music is attached directly to my soul. It is a mood-changer, an encouragement to my spirit, and a calm yet exciting space for me. Good music takes me to another place. My favorite old school hip-hop songs are Slick Rick's *"Children's Story,"* LL Cool J's *"Rock the Bells,"* Run DMC's *"King of Rock,"* and Salt 'N Peppa's *"Push It."* We experienced the best time in music. If you were able to experience hip-hop in this era, I am sure you felt blessed and highly entertained. My passion for music continued to grow over the years and continues to grow today.

While in high school, I was offered a job to work at a local community daycare center, GC Academy, which was Black-owned and led by the most beautiful and talented couple, Mr. and Mrs. G. GC Academy and its owners were a pillar of the Syracuse community and positively impacted so many lives in their time. I am honored to say that I have encountered such amazing people and had an amazing experience there, where I mentored and oversaw its after-school students while I was a high school student in the 11th grade.

It is interesting how my role as a big sister prepared me for a position that involved working after school each day with children whom I absolutely enjoyed mentoring and guiding at GC Academy. I strongly believe that having younger siblings prepared me for this time with an assignment of working with the lovely and intelligent children who attended this divine educational institution. Although I was an after-school *"teacher,"* I was also a learner because GC Academy's program included a wealth of education that also incorporated African and African American history within its curriculum, and it was taught in such creative ways. The directors made it fun and exciting to learn important facts and details of our very own at a time when African and African American history was sparsely taught in public schools.

GC Academy's educational structure was outstanding and uniquely designed to teach children not just the basics of learning but the knowledge of their rich African and African American history, legacy, and culture. The students were taught about Black historical figures and change agents in various knowledge base areas, ranging from inventors to political leaders to community activists who pushed for and created positive changes in Black communities and in the world. The curriculum included unique musical role-playing and storytelling that were shared with the students with love and grace. The teachings also included a priceless experience that captured impressionable age children with the most important tools needed to be self-aware and self-confident in who they are as people of color, along with showing them and teaching them what pride looks like. This educational structure groomed the children as individuals who were encouraged to be anything that they desired to be in this world.

My experience working at GC Academy was top-notch, and it granted me knowledge and exposure that I would not have learned from my day-to-day coursework in high school at that time. I am thankful that I received the opportunity to work with our adored community youth while I simultaneously learned as I helped in my own way, to teach the knowledge of rich African and Black American history. I was empowered and encouraged, and the gaps that may have been open in my traditional education experience were filled through this opportunity. I enjoyed and embraced the chance to lead, encourage, and nurture the youth in my community. It was such an all-round fulfilling and empowering experience. I would do it all over again if asked to do so.

As a high school student, I was quiet, yet I connected with like-minded classmates who had similar goals. We were college-bound and enrolled in classes and programs that prepared us for our college journey. I also joined Xi Chapter youth group named Kopelles, a high school organization that was based on sisterhood, academic excellence, and community service. When we influence the youth with the importance of unity and service early on, we build up a community and a nation to withstand anything that adversaries may attempt to place on or over us.

Serving others with purpose builds villages and communities that can stand strong even in the most difficult times. Around the same time as joining Kopelles, I was active in my church, Pentecost EMB church under my bonus grandfather, Reverend (Grandpa) Joseph, who was the father of my bonus father, Tony. Tony was caring and supportive of us. He and my mother brought us to church with them every Sunday. This type of exposure planted seeds in us as children. Proverbs 22:6 says, *"Train children how to live right, and when they are old, they will not change."*

My maternal grandmother, Lucille, was a strong woman of God who would visit us from Georgia in the summer, and when she visited our church, she had a beautiful testimony to share with the congregation every single time. Her testimony often ran well over the delegated window of time and required some nudges signaling to wrap it up, but her love and honor of Christ flowed like a river, and we all felt it.

Grandma Lucille could talk the entire day about the Lord and His goodness in her life. This was such an inspiration for me as a youth to directly witness my grandmother's passion for Christ and to see how spirit-shifting her testimonies were for us listeners. So, as the head of households and followers of Jesus Christ, we have a duty to introduce our children and grandchildren, our legacy to Jesus Christ.

Acknowledgment of our Father, God, and His son Jesus Christ is the most important relationship and partnership we can have as a resource while maneuvering through life, contributing to a world where this relationship will guide us as a compass in initiating positive and healthy changes needed in our households, communities, and the entire world.

This relationship will encourage us to submit our individual steps to be ordered by God. There is no better fulfillment than walking in the individual purpose that our Father has designed for each of us.

As a young teen with such a heavy influence around me, I became deeply inspired to lead my future children and grandchildren to Jesus Christ just as my parents and grandparents had done for me. Leading them by example is the most important action as it applies to me.

At the age of 15, I gave my life to Jesus Christ, and I was baptized in the water. John 3:5, *"Jesus answered, I tell you the truth, unless a man is born of water and of Spirit, he cannot enter the kingdom of God."* Getting baptized was very important to me. I still remember the beautiful experience as if it happened yesterday. I remember wearing my swim cap (to prevent the water from seeping into my relaxed 4C hair) as my pastor, Grandfather Joseph, submerged me into the water backward and quickly lifted me back up out of the water. My spirit felt refreshed, and it basked in an indescribable peace. It was a peace that was consumed with pure love and joy. The weight of my surroundings felt feather-light, and all of us who were baptized that day felt God's presence among us.

There is no other experience like baptism, as it is overall life renewing, and it brings us to a deeper connection with a renewed commitment in following and honoring our Lord and Savior, Jesus Christ. In Matthew 28: 19-20, Jesus instructs his disciples to baptize new believers in the name of the Father, the Son, and the Holy Spirit (Abundant Life, https://

livingproof.co). It is very important for us to make the beautiful and most powerful choice of receiving Jesus Christ as our Lord and Savior through baptism. I encourage everyone to try Jesus and to show the world how important it is for us to show our commitment to Jesus in following Him and His church and carrying the cross wherever we go. No one is perfect. However, we serve a perfect God, and I am here for it whenever the opportunity permits me to glorify His name. Anytime is always a great time to speak about the goodness of God.

CHAPTER

Two

High School Senior Year Fun: Lessons, and Meeting My First Love

My senior year high school experience was deeply entrenched with homework and projects as I juggled courses such as Advanced English, college Biology that was administered through Syracuse University, pre-calculus, my job at the day care center, community service activities, applying to colleges, preparing for the prom, and senior graduation. Also, I couldn't forget my little social life with my high school friends who were just as busy as me, if not busier. Many of them were affiliated with other organizations, such as the NAACP local youth chapter and its ACT-SO competitions, which were outstanding.

One of my best friends won first place for the oratory scholarship that year, and we were so proud of her. I enjoyed the blessing of befriending like-minded students, and because of this our goals were similar, we were able to assist and encourage each other in our studies and endeavors, making our educational journey a smoother path. I was always inspired by my circle of high school friends, which gave me the drive to walk in excellence just as they did.

My senior year photoshoot was great, and I must say I looked amazing. My Aunt T prepped me for my special pictures with my hairdo and makeup. I had two outfits that I picked out to change into, as I prepared to take my senior year school pictures. I wanted the pictures to be beautiful yet serious, fun, and represent a classy and educated appeal. I wanted my senior pictures to represent me well, and the photographer navigated the photoshoot in the way that I had envisioned. Once I received my picture portfolio, I shared copies with friends and family. I shared one with my closest friends and my best friend, Ki, and she placed the magnet copy that I gave to her on her refrigerator at home.

One day, as Ki and I were in school, she told me of her cousin, VP, who visited them during the weekend. She told me that he saw my picture on her refrigerator and he told her that he wanted to meet me. Ki then handed a written letter to me from VP, and I was surprised by the gesture. I decided to read the letter when I got home that evening after work. It stated how he saw my picture on the refrigerator at his cousin's house, how he thought that I was cute, and wanted to meet me in person. He added his phone number to the letter so that we could have an initial conversation. This was different for me because my head was deep in my books, and the thought of trying to start dating with my crazy schedule and full workload would be insane. Plus, I was going to head off to college in another town soon.

I've seen VP at various events in town in the past, but I did not know him personally. He was most definitely handsome and muscular, but I was super quiet, shy, and a *"skinny-mini."* I already had my own little routine that did not incorporate dating. I had male friends in school, but that was all, nothing more than just friends.

VP and I were *"night"* and *"day."* We were like Popeye and Olive Oil. VP was a very persistent individual. I enjoyed our conversations, and so we began to talk on the phone often and set up time to meet at different locations, such as the popular mall or the teen club, to hang out. As we began to learn about each other as friends, we became closer. The more we hung out together, the closer we became. We enjoyed the process of learning about each other, our similarities and our differences (which were a lot). I was beginning to really embrace this new friendship. I continued to make school a priority, especially since my plate was full and I needed to ensure that I met deadlines and prepared for exams. I remained closely connected to my girlfriends, enjoying all that my senior high school year brought, while also managing my *"to-do"* list accordingly. I was able to maneuver through my senior year successfully. My girls and I were on the same page, meeting and beating our goals. We were all on track and making room for the fun part of our senior year, and welcoming all the excitement that the last year in high school offered. With that, we not only worked hard in our studies. We also played hard and enjoyed a good party with good music whenever we could get into the venue (wink-wink).

In our downtime, my friends and I enjoyed exploring the Syracuse University campus and the various activities and parties that were offered to the community students. The annual Greek Freak hosted on the Syracuse University campus by its National Pan-Hellenic Council was a local and national *"go to"* every spring when the Divine Nine (Greek organizations), students and locals came together to party, attend concerts, eat good food, socialize, and watch stepping competitions among all the sororities and fraternities across the country that represented each organization.

The stepping performances always blew my mind as the participants would get more creative each year with their delivery and custom-made uniforms. The step masters showed out by orchestrating their unique flow and movements to the latest beats that were in rotation for that year. The music was always on point and kept the crowd moving. Visiting the campus gave us a preview of the college life experience, and we always had a great time. In fact, my friends and I enjoyed ourselves in our downtime so much that we took the three-and-a-half-hour drive to Manhattan, New York, to have our New York State driver's license photo IDs made to our personal liking about two or three weeks before the event. We were able to order our preferred date of birth, name, height, weight, and address. We enjoyed music and dancing, and this was what gave us our *"high"* and *"fix"* when we were out on a night in town.

My high school friends and I had a passion for music as it penetrated our souls in such a good way. Hip-hop, R&B, reggae, and House music were our favorite genres at that time in the 90s, and so when the beat dropped, we all hit the dance floor.

Getting into an event or *"the club"* was all about enjoying a space where good music, great conversation, and even better company came together. I recall one time and one time only (as I laugh with this memory) when I begged my mother to allow me to attend one of the parties on the Syracuse University campus with Ki. She mentioned that if I had a ride back home, I could go, but only if I had a ride back home locked in. So, one of our upperclassmen (or should I say a big brother) told us that he would drop us back home once the party was over. When this was confirmed, I received the green light from my mother to attend the party. My best friend and I were so hyped about going and having a great time.

The school week seemed to go by slowly, and when Friday finally arrived, we made it to the party on campus that evening. We could hear the music thumping as we walked up to the front door entrance.

The place became jammed-packed really quickly. The music inside was bopping, the crowd was dancing, while sorority and fraternity members strolled throughout the space. The mood was just right, and we did our thing on the makeshift dance floor, and before we knew it, three hours had gone by. We were having so much fun! The music was good, so good that my friend and I decided to go to the after-party too.

The after-party was great, and when the party hype wore down, we were ready to go home. We went to our upperclassman's friend to ask if he would drive us home, and he stated that he was not ready to leave the party. We asked another friend there who owned a vehicle, and the answer was also *"no."* No one wanted to leave the after-party to take us, high school students, back home, off campus. After waiting for almost two hours, someone agreed to drop us off at home. By then, it was close to 4 a.m., it was way past my midnight curfew, daylight was trying to catch up with me, and the birds were prepared to shake their heads at me at that point.

That walk of shame from the car to my front door was super long. I quietly slipped inside the house. I tiptoed to the foot of the steps leading to my bedroom when I heard some movement going on upstairs. I hurried over to the recliner and lay back on it, pretending to be asleep. As I was lying down in the recliner, my mother quickly walked down the stairs and said to me, *"Why are you just now making it home at 4 a.m.? You were supposed to be home by midnight!"* I was at a loss for words because I already knew what was about to go down at this point. Nothing was about to go down; I was going to be allowed to do *"nothing"* starting right now.

My mother went on to say, *"I told you that you had to be home by midnight, and if you did not have a ride home, you could not go!"* I explained to her that someone had agreed to take us home, but at the time we needed to leave, they were not ready to leave the party. That answer did not fly with my mother. She had already made up her mind, and that was final. As I walked over to the steps to go upstairs, my thoughts were all over the place because I just knew that this was going to be a very long punishment, and without any room to negotiate. I was convicted and guilty of the charge. I knew at that moment that I would have to kiss attending that year's annual Syracuse University Greek Freak goodbye.

I was on punishment for a month, and I could only attend school, work, church, and my bedroom. It was a very long month, and I literally cried because I was going to miss one of my favorite events of the year that all my friends were planning to attend. I begged my mom for mercy as the time became close to the big day, but her answer remained *"no"* because it was a lesson that I had to learn in this situation. I learned quickly and immediately, and decided to plan my future parties or outings mindfully, or I would plan to bow out of the plans if they were not in line with the rules of the house. I knew that I would not be attending the Greek Freak that year as a result of making it home after my curfew, which was just not worth it.

From the perspective of being a mother now, I can understand the importance of tough love in protecting and guiding our children by making sure that they abide by the rules surrounding curfews and being responsible. As a mother, I can most certainly understand the importance of holding not only myself, but also my children accountable for the things that I entrust them to do in ways that are for their good and safety. My mother's firmness in this matter was that of love and protection, and I respected that. I also emulated this same mindset later on with my own children.

VP and I met around the time of my senior prom. He had graduated the year before and attended his prom at a different high school. He wanted to escort me to my senior prom. However, when we formally met just a few months before, I already had plans to attend the prom with AH, who was friends with my cousin, GG. GG planned to attend the prom with my friend Ki. I loved the idea of this, and we all were looking forward to a classy time and experience. So, we all went to the prom together as a double date.

I asked my neighbor and family friend, Mrs. Char, who was an avid sewer, to make my prom dress. I chose a rose-pink mermaid cut dress with heels the same color as my dress. I ordered white heels from Payless ShoeSource, and I had my new white heels dyed rose-pink. I wore pearls for jewelry, and my Aunt T did my make-up and helped me curl my hair. At the time, I had a short, tapered (layered) haircut.

In the 90s, all the girls and women wanted the beautiful *"Halle Berry"* haircut. I have thick, coarse hair (4C hair), so a perm relaxer was a must for me during that time because my hair could not withstand any moisture. AH wore a black tuxedo and a rose-pink cummerbund to match my dress. He looked sharp, dapper, and handsome. Ki and GG wore a berry or burgundy color and a black combination. They looked wonderful and very much complemented each other.

Our senior prom started off rocky when the key to GG's uncle's Porsche snapped inside the door lock while the guys were out grabbing last-minute items. That was supposed to be our ride. The delay pushed back the tuxedo pickup, and suddenly we were running very late. After more than an hour of stress and no access to the Porsche, we ended up going to prom in my parents' 1989 Dodge Caravan. I was not happy, and neither was anyone else. So much for arriving in luxury and style.

We missed the sit-down dinner but made it in time for pictures, dancing, and games. Surprisingly, it turned into a better-than-expected night. I enjoyed the double date and especially the DJ spinning all the blazing hits. I danced with my date and even wiggled in my seat. I was fully in my element. I've always been a *"music head,"* and there's something about the 90s to early 2000s hip-hop and R&B, the Golden Age, that still holds me.

Then I spotted VP across the room, dancing to one of the hottest tracks of 1991, *"You Can't Play with My Yo-Yo"* by Yo-Yo featuring Ice

Cube. He had come as a guest with his cousin and best friend, JH, who was in my social studies class. Even though I had my own date, VP made sure his presence was felt. He carried himself like someone who follows through, and I liked that. He and JH looked sharp and brought a noticeable energy to the room.

My date and I took pictures and danced, while Ki and GG did the same. We all looked beautiful and truly enjoyed the night, especially with a rare pass from my parents that freed me from worrying about curfew.

Once prom was over, reality set in: the transition to college. I applied to ten schools, Syracuse University, University of Pittsburgh, Hampton University, Howard University, State University of New York at Buffalo, State University of New York at Albany, Pennsylvania State University, Hempstead University, and State University of New York at Stony Brook, among others. I had hoped to attend an HBCU, and I was accepted into all ten. However, due to limited financial aid, I chose a state school for affordability.

I ultimately enrolled at the State University of New York at Buffalo (SUNY Buffalo), where in-state tuition made a top-quality education more accessible. As the flagship public research university in New York, it offered an incredible opportunity, and I was grateful to begin that next chapter there.

As a high school senior, my guidance counselor (the best high school guidance counselor ever), Mrs. D, continued to guide me in the direction of my future education plan, and she also introduced me to an internship program named INROADS, which is a corporation where leading industry companies sponsor college-bound students with a competitive salary and an on-the-job experience during their college career. In addition, there were also opportunities to establish a career with a corporate sponsor company upon the end of the four-year internship program and college graduation. I signed up for an information session that the INROADS team had at my high school. I was very impressed and wanted to be a part of this distinguished organization. I was able to apply to participate in the program and was accepted.

The next step was to apply to corporations that would be a great fit for me to learn, grow, and contribute to as an intern and future full-time employee. I interviewed with United Technologies Carrier Corporation in East Syracuse and was selected as one of their interns, where I initially worked in the IT and Business Management departments through the INROADS internship program. This experience was unmatched as I established a wealth of key knowledge and skills through hands-on learning and applying the knowledge learned. This experience provided me with a platform on how to navigate the corporate world as a young, educated woman of color. The unique skillsets that I learned through being an intern prepared me for success in any corporate space once I completed college.

According to the INROADS Heritage Center, *"It was at that time that Frank C. Carr, our late founder, planted the seeds for what INROADS has become today. Inspired by Dr. Martin Luther King Jr.'s landmark 'I Have a*

Dream' speech, Frank quit his executive-level corporate day job and committed to taking swift and decisive action to increase ethnically diverse employees in corporate management in the U.S. and to help change the way these candidates gained entry into the business world."

INROADS centered its mission around diversity and inclusion in the workplace over 50 years ago, with the mindset of equal opportunity and the ability for people of diverse backgrounds to experience corporate success through their unique skillsets and experience, thereby bringing a well-rounded and competitive workforce with limitless growth and success. The regular weekend workshops that INROADS facilitated fully trained and prepared us for success at any corporation. The training ranged from how to dress and present yourself in business environments, to time management and assertiveness skills, to effective public speaking techniques.

INROADS developed greatness in its program and helped to produce successful entrepreneurs with breakthrough inventions, CEOs of Fortune 500 organizations, and powerful business leaders and executives throughout the world. Being affiliated with such an amazing organization was life-transforming and has continued to impact my life in many ways as I navigate my personal and professional journey.

I thank God for His goodness and His grace in connecting me with destiny helpers who assisted in preparing the way for me and led me toward my purpose in my education and my future career endeavors.

Samuel 25:32-35(NIV) says, *"David said to Abigail, 'Praise be to the Lord, the God of Israel, who has sent you today to meet me. God will send those that He assigns to us to guide and to help us and to meet us where we are. He will send those that He equips with everything needed to build what He has called them to build for His kingdom."*

INROADS Upstate New York's leadership team, my peers, and our corporate sponsor, United Technologies Carrier Corporation, played a major role in shaping my path. Their influence helped launch me into life-changing opportunities in the corporate world.

SUNY Buffalo was an incredible place to earn my bachelor's degree. I majored in Political Science and took many English-focused courses with plans to minor in English. I started out interested in computer science, but I shifted my focus because I wanted to become a lawyer. That was my plan. But as Proverbs 19:21 reminds us, *"You can make many plans, but the Lord's purpose will prevail."* My life unfolded according to His plan, not mine.

I've learned that when things don't go as expected, staying grounded in prayer and aligned with God's will matters most. Scripture became my guide, Psalm 119:105 says, *"Thy word is a lamp unto my feet, and a light unto my path."* Even with life's detours, God directs us toward our true destination. Through prayer, obedience, quiet reflection, and fasting, I found clarity and spiritual direction.

My high school graduation was unforgettable. My entire family showed up, parents, siblings, cousins, aunts, uncles, and grandparents.

My Grandma L and her brother, Uncle R, even traveled from Georgia, which meant so much to me. They gifted me a television that I later took to college, along with monetary gifts that helped support my transition.

It was a bittersweet moment. I was excited for the future, but it was hard leaving behind people I had seen every day for years, some since middle school. Still, I felt proud of us all. Some were heading to college, others to work, and some were taking time to figure things out. No matter the path, we had all worked hard to reach that milestone, and that made the moment truly special.

CHAPTER

Three

The Transition into Adulthood, Womanhood, and Motherhood

I was happy that I decided to attend SUNY Buffalo in the fall of 1991. The great part about this was that there were many of my high school friends who also selected SUNY Buffalo that year. This aspect made the transition process a lot smoother for me and for them, too. I was roommates with two of my closest high school friends, Ki and LF, during the time I lived in the dorm, and two years later, I became a resident advisor for a year, which significantly reduced my room and board costs.

I met a wealth of other college students from across the state of New York, predominantly from the New York City area. I enjoyed the social and educational experience, as it was important for me to manage both very well because the transition from high school to college started somewhat difficult. It was a newness that I had not expected. I missed the part where I was responsible for balancing my own time that consisted of school work, work study, participating in college-related activities, and, of course, the social aspect of college. I thought that I had it under control. However, I took on more classes than I could manage and did it with everything else outside of schoolwork. With that, I straddled the fence with my grades in the first semester of my freshman year, and I needed to learn to adjust and balance my studies and social life more effectively. Unfortunately, I was way too in awe that we did not have a curfew at our freshmen dorms, and learned rather quickly that in college, there is no one keeping track of your curfew and whereabouts, or how often you are studying.

I learned the difficult way that it is the student's choice and responsibility to ensure that he or she attends classes and to practice self-discipline because the decisions that he or she makes for his or her education do not affect the instructor in any way, shape, or form. The decisions you make will only impact you. The instructor will still receive his or her paycheck for instructing, whether I pass or fail is what eventually sank in my thoughts.

I socialized myself into a less-than-acceptable first-semester freshman year grade report. I was disappointed with this outcome and my not-so-great decision-making, so I had to immediately get myself together to refocus. I learned to prioritize better and to set aside a specific amount of time to study and do it all with balance as I adjusted as a new college student. Despite the rough start, my overall college experience was priceless. The learning experience, the social aspect, the on-campus and off-campus events, friendships, opportunities, personal growth, etc. I met some amazing people who later became lifelong friends. My best friend, LH, whom I met in college, later became my son's godmother. I was the maid of honor at her wedding, and we remain the best of friends today. I have two other friends that I attended college with who remain friends with me today, and they also live in Georgia.

The professors or instructors at SUNY Buffalo were awesome and went above and beyond my expectations. The course in which I had the most enthusiasm was English. I simply love the art of the English subject. One of my favorite English professors, Mrs. Polite, taught English so passionately and gracefully. One day, when we arrived in her class, she was not in attendance. We were very surprised because she never missed a class. The entire class was bummed as we looked forward to her presence, creativity, and expertise each week. The following week, she was present, and she shared with us that she was absent because she could not miss attending the ceremony for her cousin, Toni Morrison, receiving the Nobel Prize in Literature in 1993. Of course, that was a great and extremely valid reason for being absent that day. Supporting her cousin in such an honorable accomplishment was very gracious. I feel honored to have been taught English by one of the best to ever do it.

In college, I was active in different student organizations, ranging from the Black Student Union to the general student assembly that governed a student body that numbered over 30,000. I felt that it was important to be well-rounded, to be balanced in life, and to contribute to making a positive difference in our university community. There was a wealth of events and speakers that the leaders of the organizations had invited to speak. LF, my college roommate of two years and close friend since ninth grade, was the president of the Black Student Union. She led the organization with strength, intelligence, and boldness. Through meetings and events, she empowered and educated us all and invited guest speakers who were making a powerful and positive impact within African American culture, the root of Black history, and the present state of African Americans and people of color at that time. To name a few that we received the honor to meet and hear speak were Dr. Cornell West, Sistah Souljah, Digable Planets, and the list goes on.

During my college breaks, I returned home to Syracuse to spend time with family and to work in my internship at UTC Carrier Corporation. VP seemed to always know when I was visiting home and while I was on break from college. It was like he had some internal clock connected to my daily planner. We didn't even have cell phones then. However, he always remembered my home phone number by heart over the years. Whenever I was visiting town from college, he would call and ask if I wanted to hang out with him. It was always a yes response. So, oftentimes, we will go to the mall, somewhere to eat, or hang out with relatives.

Meeting his mother was both nice and funny; her unfiltered truth had me laughing. I had already met his oldest sister years earlier in our high school Spanish class, so I knew her before I ever met VP.

VP and I started as friends, though he was persistent about wanting more. That made me nervous. I was quiet, reserved, and comfortable staying in my small circle, while he was popular and well-known in town. I also held firm to my decision to wait until marriage before becoming physically intimate, a mindset I carried with me into college. I enjoyed laughing and having fun, but I stayed grounded in my choice to remain abstinent. Peer pressure can be intense, especially for young people, but being firm in your values helps you stay committed to your beliefs and actions. I refused to let anyone define me or put me in a box. I valued who I was and built genuine friendships rooted in mutual respect, something I believe is essential, because without it, any relationship is bound to crack.

Over time, VP and I grew closer and enjoyed each other's company, whether we were talking on the phone or spending time together. While I made new friends in college, I always kept my education as my priority.

One winter, during Christmas break, a few days after I returned home, VP called me from the local county jail. He explained he had to serve a couple of months related to having a gun in his possession. That season, which we usually spent together, was suddenly very different. He asked me to visit him. I didn't want to go through the process of entering the facility, but I also wanted to see him, so during those few weeks home, I made time to visit. By then, we had built a close bond over the past year and a half.

During that time, I learned things I hadn't known before, like the fact that he had children. At that stage in my life, I wasn't open to dating someone with children or being part of anything complicated. This friendship began to feel different, and I was upset that he hadn't been upfront. At the same time, I remained focused on school. I also realized, unexpectedly, that I might have begun to love him.

Then a cousin of mine, who was visiting someone at the same facility, told me that someone else had been visiting VP while I was away at college. That was a turning point. I told him he needed to choose between the other person and me, or I would remove myself completely. I was fully prepared to walk away, especially because important details had been withheld, even though we didn't have an official label.

We eventually had a serious conversation. He told me he loved me, and I told him I loved him too. He said he would do what he needed to do. It was a lot to process, unexpected, complicated, and deeply emotional.

After a week or so, I returned to college for the new semester, and I was busier than ever. I did my best to remain dedicated to my studies and assignments. Balance was the key. VP was released a couple of weeks later. I was at a turning point because I always envisioned myself dating someone who did not have children (that was my thought and expectation for my life at that time, at only 20 years old). By this time, I had already grown a strong bond with him. I must admit that I was frustrated learning certain information AFTER the timing of our close connection. I felt that this was something that I had to give myself the time to think about regarding the situation. I had a lot going on, and I had a lot to consider concerning all that was on my plate at that specific time, as well as for my future.

About a month went by, and it was a typical school day with classes. I was at my work study location, where I completed hours in the Political Science department on the Amherst Campus. That afternoon, I received a call from one of the other resident advisors, and they called to inform me that someone was at the Main Street campus looking for me. She gave the person the phone to talk to me, and it was VP. I must admit, I was pleasantly surprised. I was missing him, his big personality and smile. I quickly finished my work and headed to the Main Street campus. When I got there, he was just hanging out and talking to the other students in the dorm lobby area. We gave each other a huge hug and kiss once we saw each other. I had some butterflies going on, yet I was so happy to see him and to spend some quality time with him.

VP's father, Mr. V, and his stepmother, Mrs. F, lived in Buffalo as well, so he was able to visit them while in town before he made it to my dorm. Mr. V and Mrs. F were wonderful, and I will never forget how they and VP's three gorgeous younger sisters loved on and helped VP Jr. and me during our time in Buffalo. I will also never forget how I met Mr. V. I was a new student at the college a couple of years prior and attended an event that had vendors present, selling lots of nice urban wear clothing at our

North Campus location. I saw this man who was the spitting image of VP. I had not yet been introduced to him by VP at that time, but when I saw him, I immediately saw VP in him. So, I had to go over to him to ask him if he had a son named VP, and when I did, he said yes. I was flabbergasted. The gene pool is very strong in that family!

I told Mr. V that I was a friend of VP's and that it was nice to meet him. I loved when Mr. V and his mother, Mrs. B, would reach out to me to see and spend time with their grandchildren when they were visiting Syracuse. They showed my children such great love, and I am so appreciative of them and the love they had for their children, grandchildren, and great-grandchildren. They were both such beautiful souls, and we miss them dearly.

During VP's visit, we talked and hung out, he met some of my friends, and we ordered something to eat. We had some deep conversations and watched movies. He was able to stay overnight at the dorm since I had my own room at the time as a resident advisor. We had a great time laughing and hanging out that evening. It was hard to see him leave to go back to Syracuse. VP was constantly on my mind, and I was always so excited to see him and to spend time with him. At this point, I felt closer to him now more than ever.

I finished the school semester in May and returned to Syracuse for the summer. I also returned to my internship with United Technologies Carrier Corporation, which I truly enjoyed. I spent time with family, friends, and of course, VP. We spent a lot of time together when I was not working. Balancing both was difficult because the summer break was a time to relax and have fun, but, in my situation, it was critical to maintain my commitment to my responsibilities. So, I learned to master juggling both business and fun.

I spent quite a bit of time with VP. He had taken me out on a date to Sylvan Beach on Memorial Day, where we had a great time driving the water-bumping cars, walking along the beach, and eating some good amusement park food. This date was much different from the norm of what we did when we hung out in the past, and I believe that it officially confirmed our feelings for one another, creating an unspoken bond and creating a memory that remained with us. I continued to move forward with this relationship despite the possibility of getting my heart broken. This young man showed me deep love; he was smart, charismatic, talented, and handsome. He was at this point deemed my first love.

As time progressed, I broke my promise of saving myself before marriage. This was my very first time being physically intimate with VP or anyone, for that matter. Making this decision was not what I had planned for myself. It just happened. It was a huge crossroad for me. About three or four weeks later, I noticed that my cycle had not arrived. So, I was assuming that it was because of stress from work for whatever reason. After missing my cycle for the second time, VP and I decided to go to Planned Parenthood to speak to someone about taking a pregnancy test.

I had not mentioned anything to anyone except VP because I was nervous and trying to digest it all mentally and emotionally. I was very worried. I took the pregnancy test at Planned Parenthood and had to wait 24 hours to call the doctor for the outcome. It was a very long 24 hours.

The next day, I stayed home from work and VP, and I called Planned Parenthood for the results. The doctor confirmed that the pregnancy test came back positive. I began to cry because I did not know what I was going to do. I felt so overwhelmed and confused because we used protection. VP was behaving calmly when the doctor confirmed the positive result. All I could think about was not being able to complete college and fulfill the goals that I had in place for my life. I continued to cry. Honestly and regretfully, I considered terminating my unborn baby. VP said he was going to support the decision that I was making, but his actions reflected otherwise. He was very quiet with me. I reluctantly called Planned Parenthood to schedule an appointment to terminate my pregnancy. When they told me of the cost, I was concerned, and so I asked VP to assist me. He said that he would, but I did not hear from him for several days. I was sad and disappointed in myself at the same time.

While out at the mall with my friends one day, I walked past a large wall mirror and as I did, I saw this young woman with a small belly pouch that reflected the obvious of her condition. I had been in denial for months. As time went by, termination would be very difficult at the local level. I would have had to travel out of my area to have the process completed. With heavy thoughts and prayers, God spoke to my heart. Proverbs 2:3-8 says, *"Cry out for insight, and ask for understanding. Search for them as you would for silver; seek them like hidden treasures."* I needed God to hold my hand and direct my thoughts and steps through this difficult process.

Seeking God's guidance in every situation is very important to me. He is my compass, my guide, and my all in all. He had never failed me, and I knew that he would not fail me now. I chose to continue with my pregnancy despite all that I had going on and where I was at that time in my life.

Meanwhile, my sister and other family members were already informed by VP that he and I were expecting. The only person that was left for me to inform was my mother. I was so nervous that she would be so disappointed in me. I was almost done with college, and here I was, pregnant. After talking to my aunt about the matter, she told me to talk to my mom and to not be nervous. I was nervous anyway. But I had to do it. My aunt also informed me that some other people were aware of my pregnancy as well and were waiting to see if I was going to stay in college or drop out.

Dropping out of college was never an option for me. It literally never crossed my mind. I finally sat down with my mother to inform her of my pregnancy. She was calm regarding the news, and I was thankful for that. I was not perfect in my actions, but I knew that I could lean on my perfect God for direction and re-direction in my current situation.

As I progressed forward, I knew that I had to have a plan in place, given that terminating my pregnancy was not an option. So, I called Planned Parenthood again, but this time my call was to schedule an appointment for my pregnancy confirmation. I went to my appointment about a week and a half later, and they examined me. Because of how far along I was and how clear the sonogram had shown, the doctor was able to confirm that I was about 12 weeks pregnant and expecting a baby boy. My entire world literally changed at that very moment. Psalm 127:3 says, *"Children are a gift from the Lord; they are a reward from him."* Every decision and action that I had taken from that point on was centered around what was best for my child.

It was not by chance that I had transferred to another college that summer (SUNY Brockport) to take some elective classes, and Brockport was much closer to Syracuse than Buffalo (about an hour and a half).

As my belly grew, I kept attending classes and continued making steady progress. I scheduled my prenatal appointments on Mondays or Fridays, which made it easier to drive home from college each weekend.

For some reason, winter was very mild that year. So, the weather did not prevent me from commuting at that time to receive my prenatal care. As I was getting closer to my delivery date, I began to make *"maternity leave"* plans with my college instructors because my son's due date was February 21st, and it was getting close to our December holiday break. I asked if I could be excused from class for six weeks and make up for all assignments given during that time when I returned. Every instructor agreed to my request, and I was so thankful for it. This saved me from having to complete an entire semester of school all over again. This situation spoke clearly to me that God will clear the path so that it is possible to do what would typically be impossible. God poured empathy into the spirits of my instructors, and I was granted what I very much needed at that time: favor and grace.

God can and will make a way out of no way. We must simply trust Him. For some of us who like to have control or are big planners of every aspect of our lives, we must learn to release these behaviors to God so that He can take the wheel and steer us on the road where He desires us to be. Being in the perfect will of God gives us the peace that surpasses all understanding. Trust me, I understand, and I understand from direct experience, it is a must to yield to His guidance, His instructions, and His plans. God does not make any mistakes.

As I returned to Syracuse from college for the holiday break, I finally had a moment to relax and prepare for my baby boy's arrival. Time was flying. VP checked on me often and helped financially when needed. He also loved making customized greeting cards from the drugstore machines, each one filled with his heartfelt words. Those cards were therapeutic, especially with my hormones all over the place and so much on my plate.

Before our babies arrived, my family hosted a double Jack and Jill baby shower for my sister TSB and me, as she was expecting a baby girl.

Our due dates were a month apart, mine in February, hers in March. The shower was full of food, music, and dancing, turning it into a true party. We received plenty of clothes and baby items, and I was also blessed with gifts from my sister-friends at college.

As I waited for my baby boy, I became anxious and went to the hospital twice, thinking it was time when it wasn't. Even on Valentine's Day, when my mucus plug came out, I thought it was time, but it wasn't. Being my first pregnancy, I learned to relax and trust God. Months earlier, I had chosen his name, Kyle Malik, after admiring Malik Yoba from *New York Undercover* and loving the name Kyle.

A few days later, my mother rushed me to the hospital early in the morning while staying in contact with VP, who was in Rochester, New York. We used beepers and phone booths, common at the time, and even relied on a friend's car phone, which felt like a luxury. It reminded me of when VP and I would drive around, listening to 90s hip-hop, R&B, and reggae without a care.

As VP made his way to Syracuse, I was terrified of the unknown. In the labor and delivery unit at CM Hospital, I could hear other women screaming. The doctor first said I wouldn't deliver until later that afternoon, but the pain quickly intensified. They gave me medication, but I threw up since my stomach was empty. I just wanted VP there. My mother supported me every step of the way. Soon after, the doctor said the baby was coming sooner than expected. Overwhelmed by the pain, I accepted an epidural.

Once we shared the update with VP, he quickly got on the highway to get to us. My baby boy was so ready to enter the world. I was zoned out from the pain medication, but it seemed as if the process began to accelerate quickly, and I had dilated far enough to begin pushing him out. It was a struggle, and I was ripped and in so much pain. He finally came out, and the nurses immediately took him into the surgery room. So, I was concerned as to why. The doctor explained to me that my baby boy had a bowel movement, meconium, while coming out of the birth canal, and so they had to take him to the surgery room to suction it out of his mouth so that he did not choke on it. My poor baby.

They finally brought him to me, and I fell head over heels in love. I was so exhausted but in love. My mother was still there, and they informed me that I had to get stitches and an episiotomy due to the ripping. On top of that, the strain from the pushing resulted in me suffering from hemorrhoids. Ouch! Ouch! Ouch!

My little body was worn out. When I learned the weight of my baby, that explained a lot. He was born at seven pounds, 14 ounces, and 20 and a half inches long. I was only 115 pounds before I became pregnant. However, all the pain that I went through was worth it. VP came rushing in, and he hugged and kissed me, made sure that I was fine before he headed straight to his new baby boy. He was so upset that he missed his baby's birth by only minutes. My baby was born with a light brown complexion, where we could see freckles all around his mouth. He had the cutest heart-shaped lips like his dad's, and he was alert and looking around the room as if he had been there before. I was blown away by the miracle of God in childbirth. Psalm 139: 13-14 says, *"For you created my inner being; you knit me together in my mother's womb."*

I was a happy and blessed new mom! My mom had left to go home to shower and rest, and I was so exhausted that I went directly to sleep. I slept for hours until the nurse came in to bring me my little one because he was crying and waking up all the other babies in the nursery. From the very beginning, this child of mine was a mover and a shaker, already showing leadership and influencing his peers (lol).

VP came back again with a couple of friends and his brother. He handed me a bouquet of roses and balloons, showing his appreciation for me giving birth to his child. The card embedded in the roses read, *"Thanks for my child!"* As I held my son and looked at him, I was thinking how much he looked like his father.

VP was adamant on us naming him VP Jr. I wanted our son to have his own name and identity. We went back and forth on this. He said that he did not want his son to be named after another man. Lol, I loved Malik Yoba and his acting skills. VP went as far as to solicit the nurse's assistance in requesting that I name our baby boy VP Jr. I was cornered, but I also thought about how much he was born to look like him and that either way, he would have his very own identity because he would be raised as such. VP said that our son's middle name had to be spelled a specific way because of how it was spelled on his own birth certificate. So, VP Jr. is the name that we agreed on, and his full name was spelled on his birth certificate the exact same way it was spelled on his dad's birth certificate.

I was tired, and as I slept, a fever crept in overnight. The nurse gave me medicine to bring down the fever, and it worked. I wanted to breastfeed, but I could not endure the pain and discomfort, so the doctor had a breast binder wrapped around me to ease the pain. So, I bottle-fed my baby. The doctor gave me medicine for discomfort and for my bottom and the stitches that would eventually dissolve on their own. The sacrifices that mothers make when giving birth were made very clear to me on the day I delivered my first child.

The baby had been taken to have his first professional pictures done in another area of the hospital, and they turned out beautiful. The next day, the nurses took my baby to get circumcised, and I felt so bad that he had to go through that painful process. I knew that it was necessary, but it hurt me deeply to have him go through that procedure. My poor baby!

The nurses showed me how to care for the area as it healed. I later went to a parenting class that was offered by the hospital for new moms, and I returned to my room afterward. On release day, VP came early to spend time with the baby and to make videos. He gathered our belongings, dressed the baby, carried the baby out, and locked his new car seat in place while the nurses wheeled me out to my mother's car, where she was waiting for us. I could not believe that I was a mother and that someone was going to call me *"mom"* from this day forward. I am so thankful for God's grace, mercy, and blessings.

While on maternity leave from college, I handled follow-up appointments for myself and the baby and had come to the realization that the course of my life has now undertaken a huge change. My baby boy and what is best for him came first from this point on. I now have someone who will fully rely on me. The Bible says, *"Train up a child in the way he should go; even when he is old, he will not depart from it."* We have read and heard this passage many times, and at this point in my life, it was time for me to practice this because it now applies to me as a parent.

VP Jr. and his presence brought out a new strength in me that I never knew that I had. There was a new transformation in my spirit, and it involved a stronger and clearer partnership between God and me if I was going to fulfill this calling of motherhood the way that God expected of me. I felt God's encouragement in me to move forward with completing my education. Dropping out of college was not an option because I needed this degree more now than ever. I desired a stable and secure future for my son. I had to put a plan in place before I could head back to college after my six-week leave. I had to cross every *"T"* and dot every *"I"* because timing was everything if I wanted to finish the semester successfully, and if I wanted to finish the semester at all.

I spoke with my aunt and uncle, and they agreed to care for my son after my six-week leave until the end of the spring semester. I planned to come home every weekend and during breaks to be with him and handle his appointments, and that's exactly how it went.

They were incredibly gracious, and I will never forget their *"yes."* They became a vital part of my village, caring for my son as their own and providing a loving, stable home while I was away at college. As hard as it was to leave him so young, I trusted them completely.

VP would also visit their home to spend time with the baby while I was at school. Their support made it possible for me to finish the semester. Without them, I might have faced serious setbacks or even had to stop my education. Timing truly mattered.

My financial aid covered my expenses, and the shorter distance made commuting easier. Even with Upstate New York's harsh winters, that season was mild, allowing me to travel safely each week. I give God all the glory: what He did for me, He can do for you.

CHAPTER

Four

My Babies Were My Reasons
to Stand Up to Adversity

I completed the spring semester and will always remember how gracious my instructors were at SUNY Brockport. I submitted my transfer to SUNY Buffalo for my final year, was accepted back, and planned to bring my baby with me.

That summer, I worked and had strong support from VP Jr., MC, his nana, and my siblings, who gladly cared for him or spent time with him. At just nine months old, MC even helped him take his first steps at her house. I was truly grateful for the village God gave me as a young mother.

As I prepared to move to Buffalo, we spent meaningful time with his father. We enjoyed a summer filled with love, spoiling our son, taking a trip to Georgia, where he met family, including my grandma, LH, and driving around Syracuse, enjoying the warm weather. We often talked about having a daughter one day, and our connection felt strong.

The day before I left for school, VP asked me to marry him. It was something I had always wanted, but I couldn't walk away from finishing college. I knew that completing my education was necessary to provide for our child and not depend on government assistance long-term. With a heavy heart, I said not now, but later. It was one of the hardest decisions I've ever made.

In tears, I returned to Buffalo with VP Jr. My uncle helped move us in his conversion van, and I rented a second-floor apartment near campus since I now had a six-month-old. Once classes began, I sometimes had to bring my son with me, but an instructor later told me that wasn't allowed. I tried relying on friends for babysitting, but our schedules conflicted, leaving me overwhelmed.

Thankfully, VP's father and stepmother, who lived in Buffalo, stepped in and cared for our baby during my evening classes. I was deeply grateful for their support. VP Jr. also bonded with his grandparents, Mr. V and Mrs. F, and his young aunties, S, B, and M. They were truly a blessing to us.

As I looked for a resolution regarding childcare for VP Jr. during my day classes, I began to get concerned. I was familiar with the area and decided to drive around the Main Street campus near where we lived. I stopped at two or three day care centers to inquire about the hours and the cost for my son to attend, and it was way too expensive for me to afford. I decided to stop at one last daycare center on Kensington Avenue, and I went inside to inquire about the details of the facility. I later learned that the day care center was Black-owned. I asked to speak with the owner, and she told me that I was talking to her. So, I explained my situation to her, and she told me that she would be willing to help me. She told me to drop the baby off on the days that I had to attend classes and that she would only charge me $50 a week for VP Jr's tuition, which covered everything for him. Hallelujah, thank you, God! My Divine Helper came through for me!

I was able to cover this expense with my financial aid refund. Had I not been given this opportunity, I would have been left with no other option but to disenroll from college. God's timing is perfect, and His grace is sufficient. I can't thank God enough for His covering and faithfulness.

The daycare teachers absolutely enjoyed VP Jr., and they would talk about how handsome and smart he was and that I dressed him so cute. They mentioned that when I dropped him off at school each day, they would look at the tag inside his shirt to see what store the outfit came from. I loved to shop for him at Baby Gap, The Children's Place, and Ralph Lauren. Although I shopped at these stores, I shopped for sales, discounts, and bargains. As mothers, we learn how to become creative and thrifty with our dollars. Coupons and sales are our best friends. I am a coupon queen. We like to look nice, and we like our children to look nice, but we do it all on a budget. Can I get an Amen?! The bonding time that I had with my son at that time was awesome. It was just the two of us, and we bonded everywhere, at home, at the laundromat, the grocery store, the park, everywhere. My baby was the light of my life, and everything that I did was all for him.

My last year in college was super busy, and I had a little one with me in addition to that, which became somewhat of a struggle. Some nights were sleepless because my baby decided that he wanted to wake up every hour. When this happened, I would still be very tired when I woke up the next morning for class. I recall crying some nights because I barely had any time to sleep, yet I still had an early morning class to make it to. Despite the lack of sleep, I still got up and got us both ready for the day. God knew my struggle, and He made a way. When God knows that our hearts are in the right place and with good intentions, He will handle the rest for us.

The first child grows with us the most as we parents learn from trial and error with our first baby. VP would come to Buffalo to spend time with us, which would ease things. I had a meeting with my counselor right before the spring semester started, and she confirmed that when I complete the spring courses, I will be ready to graduate in May. Juggling motherhood and college classes was a lot for me, but with God's guidance, I made it through one of the toughest yet one of the most fulfilling seasons of my life. Psalm 55:22 says, *"Cast your burden on the LORD, and he will sustain you; he will never permit the righteous to be moved."*

As I prepared for graduation, I was so excited to have accomplished such a milestone with God's grace and favor to credit. My family was preparing to attend my graduation ceremony and drove almost three hours to witness my big day. My mom, siblings, first niece, sister's dad, KH, my uncle J, and of course my baby boy VP Jr., were present to watch my big accomplishment, and this made my heart full. It was an amazing day! I was so blessed to have my baby boy witness me graduate from SUNY Buffalo with my bachelor's degree in political science. I felt so much excitement and a strong sense of accomplishment. God saw me through!

The family and I went to dinner afterward to celebrate my big day. After dinner, we all went back to my college apartment to prepare to move the baby and me back to Syracuse. It was *"all hands on deck"* clearing out my college apartment. My mom drove her car, and Uncle J drove the same 1989 Dodge Caravan that we rode to my prom some years ago. This van was a part of our family, too. Uncle J packed the van to its fullest capacity, and we were out of there!

Before finishing college, I was able to obtain an apartment back home that was subsidized on the east side of town, so my son and I lived there upon returning to town. Some days we would spend the night at my mom's or my aunt's house. I was happy to be done with college and back in my hometown. VP arrived at the apartment once we made it back to town the next day, and he unloaded the minivan and brought everything into the apartment, and I unpacked after he carried everything inside. I had a summer left in my internship at United Technologies Carrier Corporation.

The IT department where I began my internship eventually closed as the company decided to outsource that department a year or two prior to my graduation. So, I soaked in all that I could in my internship opportunity for that last summer, and I planned to look for a full-time job at the end of summer or early fall. I was thankful for the INROADS opportunity, as it blessed me with so much knowledge, education, and wisdom that I would not have obtained any other way. It was designed specifically for students like me, looking to learn, grow, excel, and be great contributors in all that we would do in the corporate world, leadership, and life.

The valuable details of my learning and growth through INROADS prepared me for a bright future ahead. The management team at INROADS was the dream team for us and gave us everything we needed to prosper and to excel. They showed us in their actions and commitment. They led us by example.

The summer after graduation was relaxing, and it felt good to be back home and to be closer to family. VP was traveling to and from Atlanta often, so we spent quite a bit of quality time together with our son once I relocated back to Syracuse. Around that time, he had recently lost his mom, Mrs. S, and so I poured out my best energy and comfort toward him because he was very important to me as well as his well-being. His mother's funeral service was very difficult for him and the family. I will never forget the great pain and sadness that overwhelmed us all, and so I remained focused on being there for him in the best way as he grieved.

As we all grieved. I had the opportunity to get to know his mother better since I first met her when visiting VP at their home about two years before. She and VP Jr. met after I gave birth, and she was happy to have a new grandchild join the family. She made a nice dinner and babysat the baby for us when VP and I celebrated my first Mother's Day. So she was able to receive some one-on-one time with the baby. I am thankful that my son and I had the opportunity of meeting her and were blessed with her presence. I recall her being a *"straight shooter"* and telling it like it is without any regrets. She had a big heart. She loved her babies and grandbabies and lived her life unapologetically.

After a couple of days, VP left town. The next day, while I was at work, I received a call from him informing me that he had been detained by police en route to Georgia. The call was brief. My heart sank. I did not know what to do, so I started making calls to his relatives to see if they had heard from him, if they had any additional information, or knew what was going on with him. He and his sister were very close, so I tried contacting her first. When I talked to her, she stated that she had spoken to him as well, and she had the same information as me. I was very nervous about the unknown, and all I could do was wait to find out what all this meant. I was sad, confused, and just simply worried sick. I continued to work and care for VP Jr.

VP had been away for a couple of weeks at this point, and during that time, I realized that my cycle had not come for the month of August. Maybe I was just overwhelmed and stressed, I thought. However, when I finally took the pregnancy test, it was positive. I was thinking, oh no, my son is not even two years old yet. I didn't know what was going on with VP, and so I was a nervous wreck. The next time I talked to VP, I informed him of the news. He was happy. I was stressed. Yes, we always talked about having a daughter, but I was thinking some years later down the line, after marriage, and not so soon, and not alone.

After a couple of days, I made an appointment with my doctor, and he confirmed the pregnancy. I was six weeks pregnant. All I could think about was how I was going to provide and care for two babies on my own. I completed my internship with United Technologies Carrier Corporation after the end of the summer in September, and I began to apply for permanent full-time positions with decent benefits at different companies in the area. I interviewed for professional office positions. However, being honest and informing them of my pregnancy was not the way to go. I realized that I had to just let things flow and not mention the pregnancy if I was not asked, because I was sure this was why I was not receiving job offers at that time.

My sibling's mother, MC, informed me of a company where she worked, named Deluxe, as a customer service representative. I applied for the position, interviewed, and was offered a part-time position as a customer service representative working 32 hours a week. I accepted the job and kept my government assistance healthcare coverage for my family and me since I was not considered full-time with employee benefits. I was already receiving prenatal care, and I did not want any disruption with it. VP was away for a couple of months by this time, and he always found a way for us to talk, which I appreciated. We were definitely missing him. One day, he called me and asked me to marry him again, and as much as I wanted to, I did not want to marry in this type of situation. I wanted to do it the right way, with him out and free, with him here with our kids and me. It was one of the hardest decisions that I had to make because I always wanted to be his wife and for him to be my husband. This situation broke my entire heart. Although I chose not to marry him at that time, my heart and my love remained with him.

At 23 years old, I gave birth to our daughter in the month of April, and she was born healthy and gorgeous. Vi P. (VV: her nickname) is the name that VP and I came up with. He insisted on her having the VP initials like him and her brother, VP Jr. VV weighed seven pounds and nine ounces. This time, most of the baby's weight remained with me, and so I embraced my new curves. *"No more skinny mini,"* I said to myself as I chuckled.

Baby VV came out screaming at the top of her lungs, and she was the daughter that VP and I always said that we would have one day. She was manifested by her parents. VV is her father's twin, inside and outside. I fell in love once again with the daughter that I have always desired. My sister happened to be with me earlier that day for my weekly doctor appointment when the doctor told me to go straight to the hospital from there because the baby was coming by that afternoon. VV arrived at 2:50 p.m. that day. So, I was thankful that my sister was with me to drive me to the hospital, only to have my baby girl delivered four hours later. We were all very excited to welcome baby girl VV! God shone His face on us, and we were truly blessed by His goodness. Numbers 6:24-26 says, *"The Lord bless you and keep you; The Lord make His face shine on you and be gracious to you; the Lord turn His face toward you and give you peace."*

God will carry us through any situation that may seem too difficult to handle. Our thoughts are finite, but His is infinite, so I always look to Him for what I need in any hour. The joy of the Lord is my strength. I lean on God in all circumstances, and when times become difficult, I trust that He will either move the obstacle, hold my hand as He takes me through the obstacle, or He will take me around the obstacle. So, one thing I can claim peace in is the fact that God is in control, and He has never lost a battle.

I learned that being a single parent can be one of the most trying yet one of the most enriching experiences that one will encounter. It will introduce one to the strength that he or she never knew they had. I am a witness to the struggles of doing it all alone and spreading myself so thin that it becomes super stressful at times. From what I have researched and witnessed, many Black women in America have worn this hat at some point or are currently wearing the hat of single motherhood, and this family dynamic has continued for generations in the Black community.

According to the Journal of Blacks in Higher Education's June 10, 2024 *"Black Women Are The Most Likely Group To Be Single Parents article, it states,"* The United Census Bureau has released a new report on the demographic profile of households and living arrangements in the United States over the past 50 years and the report found that the share of households made up of married-couple families has significantly dropped since the 1970s, particularly for non-White households and in 2022, only 27% of Black households were married-couple families compared to roughly 50% of White households. This data is quite alarming, and although the scale is imbalanced for many deep-rooted reasons, it reveals to us, as in culture and in race, the importance of the Black family structure and how it directly impacts not only our lives as parents but also our children who are being raised in such environments.

The key component in this is the children. Although it has been proven in most cases that it is best for children to be reared in two-parent households, there are many cases where the mother (or father)is compelled, without choice, to lead the household alone. God stirs something up in these uniquely designed daughters and sons of His. Whether the single parenthood role was by choice, by loss of partner through death, divorce, imprisonment of the other parent, or as a grandparent needing to step in as the primary parent, the position grooms one with the strength and resilience to nurture their children with a life that is structured, well-rounded, safe, and fulfilling.

We all want nothing but the best for our children, and we will make the necessary sacrifices to do so. The position and role can become challenging and overwhelming, but it develops something powerful and impactful in us. These individuals and head of households are often forced to pull the only source of strength that they have through their trust in God to come through for them to pay that light bill with the disconnection notice attached to it, for God to come through in the loan review process to get approved for a vehicle that the parent desperately needs to get themself and their children to and from work and school each day, to begging God to give her the strength to wake up and to keep going for her other children after losing a child to gun violence. I know what God can do. I have experienced His covering and His hand in my life, firsthand. Without God's grace and mercy in my life, I would not be here!

As a single parent, it is very important for one to establish a *"village"* or *"support system"* to assist them in their efforts because teamwork really does make the dream work. The old saying, *"It takes a village to raise a child,"* is very true. Having a group of people that you can trust to stand in the gap for you and your children when they are needed is priceless.

From carpooling to and from school and sports activities to babysitting and advice-giving, our villages are so appreciated and loved for all that they do, and the same sentiment is felt in return.

Realizing that I will need to press forward as a single mother with all that I had in me was the mindset that I carried as I raised my children. I did not want my children to lack in any way. I also prioritized my children by helping them to maintain the great relationship with their father that they had by taking them to visit him while he was away, so that when he returned, their bond with him would continue as usual. This is exactly how it worked out. Traveling to and from his place of incarceration was difficult to juggle at times, but the reconnection between them all upon his return remained seamless. I would not change anything about this choice, as it was such an important aspect of my children's everyday lives and their ability to receive what they needed as young children from their other parent. I did not want to hinder the opportunity for the three of them to establish and build something beautiful that always took place when they were in each other's presence. The balance from this experience produced in them wholeness and a reinforced identity. A great deal of selflessness came with this decision, and I would not change anything about it. As my children grew up to understand it all, they have expressed appreciation and gratefulness for what I had done, and I also express thankfulness in it all for the ability and mindset to do it through God's grace, mercy, and goodness.

CHAPTER

Five

Walking in Faith, Diligence,
and New Opportunities

It was important for me not to just chase my goals, but also to achieve the goals that I had placed before God by actively pursuing them. Not long after finishing college and returning to my hometown, I worked at Deluxe, a payment and data company, for four years as a customer service representative. After I worked there for three years, I dropped down to part-time because I had decided to work part-time at a local gas and light company that only had a part-time position available, but with a higher salary.

Earlier that year, I also attended real estate school on the weekends to obtain my real estate license. After a couple of months, I became a licensed real estate agent, an independent contractor when I was 28 years old, and I worked as a real estate agent alongside working my other job(s). I found the real estate business to be very interesting, as I have always had a passion for houses. I still love a house with solid bones that is well-structured and well-designed. As a realtor, I was able to assist my clients with selling and buying homes in Syracuse. It was a fulfilling experience, and I learned a great deal about the real estate industry, and I met wonderful people in the process.

I used some of the same real estate experiences later when I purchased my two homes in Georgia. I thank God for His guidance and for always preparing me for the next chapter ahead. I eventually resigned from the payments and data company to open my availability for the gas and light company that expressed an interest in offering me more hours. I was hoping to obtain a full-time position there, eventually making more money with this company over time, but it did not happen as it was not within the alignment of what God had for me.

After leaving the gas and light company, I continued to work in real estate, but I also wanted a career that included health insurance benefits, a consistent paycheck, and a position where I could incorporate my college education. It was time to switch gears. I did not want to just earn a living or to *just get by."* I wanted to have passion for what I was doing in my career, earning a solid income that would assist me in initiating a legacy for myself, my children, and my grandchildren. I wanted to grow in my skillset and knowledge in my next opportunity, and one that stimulated my growth in areas where needed.

I wanted to make an impact and a difference in what I did every day in my role. Most importantly, God wants us to be diligent workers, so diligence became a priority as I matured in my personal and professional life. Colossians 3:23-24 says, *"Whatever you do, work heartily, as for the Lord and not for men, knowing that from the Lord you will receive the inheritance as your reward. You are serving the Lord Christ."* This passage kept me centered as I expanded in my career and the roles that I worked in. This passage reminds us that the work that we do should be done with diligence and to focus on serving God in our work, career, or business, and not strictly for personal gain. I began to understand that we are called to work in a specific position at a specific company and with specific coworkers to fulfill a specific purpose that God has for us at a specific time in our lives. This is something I learned as I progressed in my career. We are not just servicing those who are constituents or customers of the business or company where we work. We are servants to our coworkers as well.

I have learned over time that when we help or assist them, we are to do it with kindness, compassion, and a positive attitude because this is what God sees as being a true servant of His. So, for those difficult individuals in work environments, I have learned to remain in character and to rise above anything less than what God expects of me as His daughter. Although it is very difficult to do sometimes when we are unfortunately provoked, discredited, or disregarded in our education, knowledge, achievements, and efforts in workplace environments, it is a must to remain in character. We also must keep in mind to never allow anyone to come between ourselves and our livelihood, how we sustain and pay our bills. That was a priority for me because some individuals can make a work environment challenging. Yet, no one or nothing is worth coming between you and the way you support your family.

In times such as these, it is important to extend grace and press forward with self-respect and a plan of action to remove yourself from the unprofessional and hostile work environment. God holds us to a certain standard and accountability for our behavior and work ethic. He will also handle those who mishandle us, His children, and in how He sees best fit. So, it is very important to yield in areas God wants us to yield and to extend grace accordingly while He contends with the situation. Keep being a positive force in every part of your life, in how you show up for others each day, and in how you receive those who show up for you.

After leaving the gas and light company, I began looking into temporary agencies in my area, and one day I received a call from Kelly Services and was informed by my agency representative that they had a position available for me that matched their experience, skillset, and education requirements. When they mentioned the name of the healthcare company, I did not recall the company at first, but I remembered that it was the same company that covered me when I was under my mother's insurance plan as her dependent. I was on board with learning and growing at a new company so that I would be able to position myself for new opportunities. The Kelly Services representative scheduled me for an interview with the hiring manager.

I went to the business office of the health insurance company, and they conducted an interview with me. I felt a sense of familiarity and peace in the interview process. The hiring manager conveyed to Kelly's representative that she was thoroughly impressed with me and loved my professional business attire and my business acumen (thank you, INROADS Upstate New York, for the top-tier business meetings, training, professional attire preparedness workshops, and the Cornell University business retreats). With that, I was offered the position at this Fortune 500 healthcare company and accepted the new role in managing credentialing for new healthcare providers and re-credentialing for established healthcare providers.

I was so excited about the opportunity and worked as a temporary employee with partial benefits under Kelly Services for two years. It was typically not the norm for temporary agencies to offer benefits to their temporary employees or contractors, but this one did in this case. The healthcare company had arranged this for individuals who were temporarily hired employees who worked with the company for two years before being considered for a permanent position (two years was the standard at that time). I was eventually hired as a permanent, full-time enrollment specialist, where I enrolled eligible children in the company's Child Health Plus and Managed Care Medicaid programs. I really enjoyed working for this organization, and it allowed me to learn about the details surrounding the private and public sectors of healthcare.

Two years later, I was promoted to Network Account Representative, and, in that role, I recruited, negotiated, and managed the contractual relationships between the company and the healthcare providers in my designated market counties in Upstate New York. I will never forget the Vice-President of our unit advising me that he selected me out of everyone else who applied because of my four-year college degree. At that time, I felt in my spirit that God used the Vice-President and this promotion to confirm that all that I endured and sacrificed to finish my four-year degree had paid off, and this was God's gift: a new position that eventually transitioned me to a new level in my career in healthcare administration. I am forever grateful to God because I was a highly determined young woman and mother, and God matched the same energy toward me and added the cherries on the top. We can't ever beat God's giving!

God has sustained me through everything that was sent to stop or to block me as I navigated this life as a young college student and young mother. He gets all the praise, honor, and glory. As David, the psalmist, says, *"His praise shall continually be in my mouth."* God is the only reason why I am here today and still standing, and I will never take this for granted.

Humility is key to me because it allows me to yield to the people and things around me, seeing the *"human"* in people and seeing them the way God sees them. Humility also allows me to view *"things"* or *"gifts"* as the blessings that God provided us in His grace. God created them all, human and things, not man. Just because He created them and shared them with us does not mean He can't take them away. This is the reason why humility is important to me. I carry humility wherever I go, and it allows God's hand to guide me where He wants me to go, and I go where He calls me to go. When our hearts and minds are not judgmental, selfish, or greedy, God gives and shows us more of Himself. I can never have too much of our God, the Most High. How about you?

As I continued to grow in my career, I began to think more about the future for myself and my children. I knew that I wanted to relocate to another city at some point in my life, and this is the primary reason why I was a licensed realtor in my hometown and had not purchased a home of my own yet. While living in Syracuse, I was considering either the Camillus, Fairmount, Liverpool, or Syracuse Valley area to purchase, as I became more familiar with the homes and the schools in the areas. My children were still young, but relocating was always a goal once I completed college. I grew up on Syracuse's south side valley area and was obviously familiar with that part of town. My support system was in Syracuse, and I valued it as it was solid and strong, and this is exactly what my children and I needed for our lives. I needed to establish a strong and solid *"village"* for my family, as the village or group of family and friends that becomes family is who we heavily rely on for support in all areas of our lives. The village or network of family, friends, neighbors, teachers, and community members supports the upbringing of a child in key areas of their lives, incorporating love, guidance, and structure. The right village will help propel a child into greatness.

My son's basketball coach, ES, and her family became a part of our village as both of our boys became best friends, and so my son made their house his second home. When our family relocated to Georgia, my son stayed at their home for the summer and visited my mom and other family members who lived in Syracuse while he was in town. I really enjoyed that, although the boys were out of school for the summer, the family still required some reading and book reports as a part of continued education while the children were on summer break. The reading and writing were key to keeping them seasoned for the months they were out of school. This is what I call balance on the basketball court and in the classroom.

I could not ask for a better family to *"village"* with. The double blessing that we later found out after meeting the family was that they were also related to VP, so the kids were technically cousins, and with that, the bond became stronger. God knows what He's doing, and He is always up to something, helping us to connect the dots and allowing individuals to cross our paths that will groom us and prepare us for the next season in our lives.

VP Jr. began to build a stronger passion for sports as he grew up, beginning with Flag Pop Warner football as a Valley Stallion at the age of five. My daughter also began as a Valley Stallion cheerleader for Pop

Warner football at the age of five. Organized sports programs have been a great resource for teaching and reinforcing self-discipline, sportsmanship, the importance of being a team player, and hard work that includes preparation and dedication. So, of course, as a mother, I had my role to play in actively supporting my children and their teammates. In some seasons, I was a team mom, where I helped to lead the team's parental support responsibilities in making sure that every player's needs were met during the season, to help share important communications to all parents, and to ensure that snacks were on hand for each child after football games.

I was the type of parent who believed that if you start something, I will make sure that you finish it. I wanted my children to know the importance of committing to something and continuing with it until completion. The exposure that children receive by participating in organized sports creates a platform for them to thrive in any environment, to understand the importance of healthy competition, lifestyle, and to understand the importance of following rules and guidelines. I am a huge advocate of organized sports and activities for children. Children will learn through such programs that hard work pays off.

As a parent, showing up to games and practices for your children offers them a sense of confidence and validation. We do not like to be disappointed, and neither do they. Our children and grandchildren will seek us out of the crowd to ensure that we are out there on the sidelines or bleachers watching them participate in their favorite sports while they are doing an awesome job and putting in the effort. Catching the highlights of the games on camera was always the goal, and simply priceless. Rewarding them felt good when they completed a job well done on and off the field. The passion that my children had for the sports and activities that they participated in helped them with their social skills among their peers and with their teachers and school staff. It gave them the confidence in knowing that they will succeed in anything they put effort into. These types of characteristics in my children have been considered a strong component for them to flourish in any environment.

Their dad, VP, was going to be released by authorities in the coming year, and he asked me three different times to relocate to Georgia with his children. I was very reluctant because I did not want to remove my children from the environment that they were already thriving in, and although I desired to relocate one day, I was hoping for our new location to be closer to the mid-Atlantic area, such as North Carolina.

I initially responded with a no twice. VP suggested that they will be fine and that this will be a better place for them to grow up, and to also have their father helping them in the process. I thought about how there were so many influential and successful Black people who lived in Atlanta and how I would love for my children to witness such greatness and be encouraged to desire the same for themselves in life, witnessing people who looked like them doing it.

At this point, VP had been transitioned into a *"halfway"* house. This is a home where people who have been incarcerated reside as they transition out of the prison system. He asked me to visit him there with his children. I chose to oblige his request as he wanted to see them and to spend time with them. We visited him there a couple of times, but one day when the children and I arrived, I proceeded to sign in the logbook for visitors, and I saw a woman's name with the same last name as VP's that was there to visit a couple of days before. I was in shock and disbelief. I was angry as I did not know what this was about, and when he walked over to his kids and me, I began to ask him a ton of questions. I was so upset and hurt to learn that VP must have married another woman while he had been away and never informed me. I was sick (sick was an understatement). I was mad at him, like how you could do this to me! How could you do this to our kids and me? I had a ton of questions and words for him! Yes, I dated at some point while he was away. However, I did not MARRY anyone else. I was so hurt! The PAIN! I cried, and I just could not believe what I had just seen and learned.

He insisted that they were not going to be together, that they were going to get a divorce, and that he was relocating to Georgia. His words were going in and out of deaf ears as I was still upset, of course, and in total disbelief of everything that transpired without my knowledge. I wondered who else knew about this and did not tell me? It took a long while for this situation to sink in because all I knew was that he asked me to be his wife, more than once, and before he went away. But now he was being released as a married man?! In fact, I was pregnant with his daughter when he went away. I delivered his daughter while he was away. I understand that I said no to marrying him when he asked me twice, but it was due to the timing of everything when he asked and not because I did not love him. Goodness gracious! I don't think that I have ever been this angry before at this point in my life!

In his defense, he reiterated that he had asked me to marry him multiple times, and that I told him *"No."* I felt that this was not a fair response because he knew why I said no, and it was not because I did not love him or that I did not want to be his wife. The timing and the place we were in our lives were not right both times. I was never informed of his marital status, which was changed while he was away. We visited him several times while he was away, so I was numb just learning this information in this way. I didn't know the other person, but I had heard of her before. However, my issue was with him, and I needed answers from him.

After a while, he talked to me about what he was in the process of doing, his situation, and his plan to move and relocate to Georgia. He said that they were divorcing. I still had a lot on my mind about everything, and the children being in the mix of this situation. The most important thing to me at this point was being able to establish a secure and stable transition to Georgia for myself and my children. I had previously initiated the relocation request process with discussions and options with the manager at my job. This opportunity was first and foremost for me, as this move would put me in a position to advance in my career and future. My mindset was that if I advanced, my kids would advance.

After I decided to relocate to Georgia, I also began working on key factors in my life, such as paying off any debt and making sure that I researched the Georgia schools and after-school programs near the Georgia location of the company where I worked. I researched apartments and the schools in that same area. My employer in Syracuse allowed me to work unlimited overtime, and this enabled me to successfully pay off my outstanding debt.

I began to work on my resume; I researched the employment market in Georgia and looked internally at my current company as a job transfer opportunity in Georgia. Initially, I had inquired with my direct manager about the possibility of working in my current role for them from home in Georgia. The answer was no. I became discouraged, but I was still determined to relocate to Georgia with employment by way of a promotion so that I could remain an employee at the company where I worked in New York for over five years. I thought that if I were hired at another company in a similar role, I would be fine with that arrangement as well. Otherwise, I was not going to move forward with the relocation process without a job already in place.

One day at work, I asked the department president in my New York market if he could help guide me toward my goal. He requested my resume, reviewed it, and marked it heavily with feedback on what to update, correct, clarify, and remove. I took his input seriously and revised every section accordingly. He then spoke with my direct manager and encouraged him to support me in pursuing an internal position within the company's Georgia market. This senior manager truly felt heaven-sent, a destiny helper. God will send the right people to assist you when your desires align with His plan.

Soon after, I checked the company's internal site and found an open account manager role in the Georgia network department, a position I had long been interested in, but that hadn't been available in New York. I applied immediately. Within two days, I received an email from the Georgia market lead requesting an interview. We met virtually, and I felt confident it went well. Deep down, I believed God was guiding my steps.

About a week later, I received the job offer. I was excited and quickly began the relocation process. I searched for housing close to the office, wanting to avoid Atlanta's heavy traffic, and found a place just ten minutes away. At 33, I moved to Georgia, leaving my children in Syracuse with my mother for about two weeks so I could get settled, secure our home, and prepare to enroll them in school as we transitioned into our new life.

I registered them to start school in New York in the interim. At that time, I also needed to adjust to my new role at my job and my new coworkers. My biggest concern was how my babies were going to adjust to the relocation and being the new kids in the new neighborhood and new schools. They were so excited to be closer to their dad. But I also knew that they had friendships and family that they had to leave behind in New York. They had relatives and friends whom they would not regularly see any longer. It was a process and transition for all of us. The two weeks away from my kids were challenging because I had never been away from them that long. It was initially a struggle learning to navigate such a big geographic area in Atlanta with minimal help offered by MapQuest at that time. Everything in the Atlanta area was spread apart by at least 30 minutes, and so it was best to know in advance where you were headed, and it was important to plan the trip out accordingly before wasting time and gas.

As for me, learning the new area and ensuring that I arrived at healthcare provider meetings on time were critical components of my job function. Although I completed contracts with healthcare providers, sometimes I needed to have face-to-face meetings with them to conduct training sessions, to discuss aspects of the healthcare contractual agreement, or if they wanted the meeting to be more in-person. I was always ready to serve in any way, should any assistance be required of me. Our leadership team updated the department's provider territory assignment list once I officially joined the team. The territories were broken out to include me in the assignment. Since I was the newest person on the team, I inherited my share of markets, with Albany, Georgia, being the farthest market from our local office in Norcross, which was almost three hours away.

I received what was assigned to me, and I ran with the opportunity and developed a great rapport with the large healthcare provider presence in Albany, Georgia, and other healthcare providers in the metro Atlanta counties that were assigned to me at that time as well. I thank God for my prior network management experience in Syracuse, as it allowed me to build on it and to grow in ways that I did not imagine. God is always, always a step ahead of us, preparing us for what is to come next in our lives.

Ephesians 2:10 says, *"For we are God's handiwork, created in Christ Jesus to do good works, which God prepared in advance for us to do."* This is why it is so important to remain in tune with what direction God wants us to take, because He will place people and situations among us so that they may influence how we make our decisions and how we handle matters that were placed on us to change, strengthen, or enrich us, and at the same time help others in these same capacities. These occurrences establish in us the characteristics that we will need to walk in our full calling or purpose in this life. Every encounter will serve a purpose for us as we are in the process of God designing us to be who He called us to be. We just need to take heed and understand that the *"good feeling"* encounters are wonderful and comfortable.

Know that the tough encounters are very difficult to bear, but God is always there to hold our hands, redirect us if needed, and comfort us in every way. He will also send destiny helpers to assist us along the way. With this arrangement, we will not fail! Isaiah 41:13 says, *"For I, the Lord your God, hold your right hand: it is I who say to you. Fear not, I am the one who helps you."* In the turbulent storms, God will show us His face. He will keep, guide, and protect us. So, whenever we experience inevitable trials and tribulations, we can most certainly trust that God will come to our rescue and save us as we look to him for help.

Psalm 121:1-4 says, *"I lift up my eyes to the mountains-where does my help come from? My help comes from the Lord, the maker of heaven and earth. He will not let your foot slip. He who watches over you will not let you slumber."* These are words of promise from the Lord, our God. When times seem to be difficult, we can seek His protection, comfort, and care. I receive complete peace in this passage where God shares this declaration to us, His children. If He can care for the birds, He most definitely cares for us as his children, and we can walk boldly and confidently knowing this fact and promise from God. He can make a way out of no way, and I speak from experience.

There is nothing that can separate us from the love of God. I met a lot of wonderful coworkers in my first two weeks in my role and at my new work location, and found the transition to Georgia to be smooth so far. While my children were still in New York, I took advantage of the opportunity to familiarize myself with the area where I will now call home. Norcross had a wealth of grocery stores, restaurants, and entertainment for me and my family to enjoy in our downtime from the daily hustle and bustle. I began unpacking, organizing, and cleaning the new place and preparing to reunite with my children in this new space of ours. I was glad that my children had the opportunity to meet their siblings on their dad's side at relatively young ages and were able to establish relationships with them prior to us relocating to Georgia. This was a blessing as they were able to remain in contact and continue to be active in each other's lives.

CHAPTER

Six

New Environment, New Home,
and God's Covering

*J*had to keep pinching myself because it had not sunk in that we were officially Georgia residents now. So far, the people seemed to be friendly. Southern hospitality was something that I could quickly get used to, and it was highly needed in my situation, where I was far away from family, friends, and what I was used to. I was missing my kiddos, and so I began planning my trip to pick them up in New York to bring them to Georgia so that they can get settled in. I called them every day to check on them and to inquire about their day. The concern of my children transitioning to Georgia smoothly and seamlessly was at the forefront of my mind. I was hopeful and worried at the same time. I was very happy that my new workplace environment was pleasant and that my new coworkers were cordial, cool, and welcoming.

I rented a four-door sedan for the drive to pick up my children in Syracuse, hoping to save on gas, leaving behind in Georgia my GMC Envoy that I purchased as my 30th birthday gift to myself as a proud moment and pat on my own back in that milestone. Shout out to my uncle, WB, my father's brother, who worked for General Motors for several years and retired from there. We are a GM family, and I was able to reap the family discount benefit for three vehicles over time. Uncle WB was a hard worker and always kept me informed on everything going on with the family after I moved away. What a blessing this was to me. What a blessing he was and still is to my family and me. My aunts and uncles are like extensions of my parents, and I love them all as such.

The drive up to New York was uneventful, steady, and safe. Thank you, God! After about six hours of driving, I stopped at a hotel overnight to get some sleep and to recharge. The next day, I made it back to my hometown to pick up my children and the remaining belongings that were left in our townhouse. My kids were just as happy to see me as I was to see them. My brother, MG, drove our one-way U-Haul to Georgia, hung out with us for a couple of days, and then flew back to Syracuse. My brother's take-charge attitude in helping my kids and me meant so much to me.

By this time, my kids were also ready for their next chapter in another state and seemed to be somewhat excited about this major change. My children had the best attitude about relocating, and I was super excited about this important factor. Although they were children, their thoughts and feelings mattered to me in this transition. I was proud of them! I wanted the best life for them with the best opportunities for them to prosper and to excel in whatever they set their mind to do.

This town amazed me with all its go-getters and successful people. I had heard they called Atlanta the Black Mecca, and I began to see why. This fueled inspiration for my family and me. If my children were in a healthy place with this major transition, so was I. As a young woman of God, I was always told by my grandparents that if I were to ever relocate to another town, to always seek the house of the Lord in my new town. So, we chose to worship on Sundays at Victory World Church, which was only ten to 15 minutes away from our apartment in Norcross.

We absolutely enjoyed everything about Victory World Church, from the way they welcomed and greeted us each Sunday to the children's ministry, to the worship service, to how they delivered the word each week. We were spiritually fed and filled with the Word, and although Victory World Church had a very large congregation, my family felt seen and valued by the congregation, and the leadership. This experience was a blessing and kept us grounded while navigating a new life in Georgia.

I really enjoyed living in Gwinnett County and was happy to enroll my son in its version of New York's Pop Warner football league. VP Jr. had a passion for sports ever since he started playing flag football at the age of five, in Syracuse as a Valley Stallion. As he grew, his passion grew for football and basketball, and he even enjoyed baseball. He played on the Norcross football team, and the parents were so supportive and were always willing to assist after we joined the league. So, when we started the program, we only needed to purchase a new helmet. The child of the gifting family became my son's first best friend in Georgia. Since my boy was happy about playing football for this new league, I was happy too.

I love how God shows up for us in ways that we least expect, in the small encounters and in the big ones. God never ceases to amaze me! School was going to begin for the year in about a week, so I had to make sure that the children had all that they needed to be prepared. School supplies, clothes, underwear, shoes, sneakers, and hair management were on the to-do list. I think I may have been more nervous about the first day of school than my children were. I was concerned about how they would be able to navigate an entire school of new people, students, teachers, and administrators. They will be the new kids from up north, and so I was praying for a smooth transition and expected the best outcome for them.

VP Jr. was entering his first year in middle school at Pinckneyville Middle School as a sixth grader (this is the first year that sixth grade was moved under the middle school umbrella, so of course, I had my *"helicopter mom"* hat on), and VV was entering fourth grade at Peachtree Elementary. VP Jr. was not feeling the *"helicopter mom"* behavior because, as a new middle schooler, that cramped his style. Ironically, VP was giving VP Jr. a haircut to prepare him for his first day of school. I looked at the result and saw that he cut VP Jr.'s hair into a mohawk. I was in a state of shock yet terrified of how the other students, teachers, and staff would receive my child as the new student, making his debut with a mohawk haircut. That was a super bold move in my opinion. Both VP and VP Jr. were pushing the envelope.

I was nervous about my son entering the new school with a different appearance from the typical low haircut-wearing young man that he used to be. Both VPs were just alike and always walked to the beat of their own drum, never concerned about what others thought about them. The first week of school for VP Jr. was a success, and the mohawk haircut was a HIT! It did not miss as everyone loved it. VP Jr.'s nickname was created by his peers and teachers at school, and he was called *"Mohawk"* from that day on. What a first impression! So, since VP Jr. was called *"Mohawk,"* VV was called *"Mohawk's Little sister."* She received the acknowledgment by default, and she was super proud of it! I was a proud mama bear and so thankful to God that they both took this major transition and new life in a new city and state by storm. I could not ask for a better reaction. I could not ask for better children.

According to L.R. Knost, *"The ultimate gift we can give the world is to grow our tiny humans into adult humans who are independent thinkers, compassionate doers, conscious questioners, radical innovators, and passionate peacemakers."* I am a mother who can walk and talk boldly about how this quote has laid the framework for the vision of me as a parent who allows God to work through my children in any circumstance they may encounter, positioning them to be leaders and positive influencers, even as youth.

The school year went smoothly, and VP Jr. did great in basketball at Pinckneyville Middle School, and VV did her *"thing"* on the court playing basketball at Peachtree Elementary. Their father and I agreed for them to enroll in an after-school program at the local YMCA, where they continued to participate in extracurricular sports and worked on their homework immediately after school. I loved the new community in which we were living. Our neighbors became family. My children also met their closest friends there and thrived as youth with peace and balance. My job was eight minutes away from the after-school program at the YMCA, so that worked out nicely. We enjoyed living there as we had family that came to visit us from out of state often, and we simply created great memories. Not long after moving to Georgia, VP gave me a beautiful diamond ring. Just out of nowhere, he gave it to me. He said that he wanted me to have it. So I wore it with care. It is true when they say that diamonds are a girl's best friend.

That late winter to early spring, I discovered that I was pregnant, I was very surprised, and I thought that I had the flu when I was experiencing lots of congestion. I continued my daily routine for a couple of weeks before I went to see a doctor, and one day, while in the bathroom at home, I miscarried at nine weeks. I was completely devastated. I was in shock. I cried tears of pain, not knowing what went wrong and what happened. This type of confusion and pain bombarded my spirit. I was taken to the hospital by ambulance, and the doctors examined me, completed bloodwork, and confirmed what I already knew. I continued to have a heavy flow for a couple of days and took a day off from work the next day, and in addition to this day, I had the weekend to recuperate. In this process, I had to hold VP Jr. and VV tight and continue to trust in God's promises that keep us in times of difficulty. Psalm 34:18 states, *"The Lord is near to the broken-hearted; he saves those who are crushed in spirit."* I needed some time to get through this difficult process as God continued to cover me with His presence.

I received a great deal of clarity in this season, and I needed to continue to make my children my primary focus and my priority over anything or any situation that may take me off course of my primary goals in the process of relocating to Georgia and getting acclimated to a new environment. I did not want to allow anything other than my priorities to consume me. I had to continue to push through and remain on track with my plans and goals.

After two years of living in an apartment, I decided that it was time to consider purchasing a house. Two years was the plan because it gave me time to learn and to adjust to the Atlanta area and to research what part of town I would view as the best fit for my family and me. Living in a county with a favorable school district and the area's safety were very important to me. We were already living in Gwinnett County, and I loved the school district there. It offered the International Baccalaureate program, in which my son participated at that time. My children were active in sports, and so, I wanted to make sure that they continued in our new area.

One day while at work, a coworker informed me that she recently went through a home buyer program through NACA-Neighborhood Assistance Corporation of America and purchased a three-level townhome in Duluth, Georgia. I was in awe of this information, and I was anxious to obtain the details from her so that I could get started as quickly as possible. At the same time, my son said that he was ready to move into a house. Talking about timing! He was vocal in expressing that he no longer wanted to live in an apartment. The neighbor in our apartment complex had just purchased a new home in Lawrenceville and was preparing to move as well. My son was good friends with their son, and so when he went with them to visit their new home before their closing, it must have sparked something in him to ask about us purchasing a new home as well. He wanted it to happen sooner rather than later.

Although the apartment served its purpose, we were never comfortable there. My children were ready to have their own permanent space with their own front and backyard. My son wanted to live in a house that he could call his own, and I completely understood his thoughts and feelings on this. I had the same desire as my son because purchasing a home was always an important goal for me to accomplish in life.

The delay in my purchasing a home sooner was that I wanted to relocate before doing so. Although I was a realtor and listed and sold homes years prior, I had not yet purchased a home of my own, and I was fine with that until the time was right. Now that I was in a more stable position professionally and personally, I was ready to take the step into home ownership. I went through the same homebuying requirement process as my coworker friend, so I was ecstatic about the benefits that were included in the process. I attended many information workshops and volunteer events through NACA and walked away full of great information about the program, its purpose, goals, and its foundation.

After completing the program, I was assigned to an NACA realtor who was great at assisting me in the process. I promised my son that we would be in our own home before he graduated from middle school. We lived in our apartment in Norcross for two years, and right before the two-year mark, we moved into our new home. The process started a little difficult because I began my search during the 2008 housing market crash. This situation was totally outside of my background and experience in the prior years as a real estate agent. Talk about bad timing!

I saw some amazing homes in the southern crescent of the Atlanta area, but unfortunately, there were some struggles with the home-buying process because many of the homes were bank-owned at the time. In a time like this, the home search process was more difficult as the banks received several purchase offers, but waited until the highest offer came through on a home. I waited days or weeks for the banks to respond to my offers just to receive notice that my offers had been declined. Initially, I became very discouraged because there was always a higher offer than mine. Most of the buyers in the market at that time were investors, so I was going up against the big ballers who did this for a living and had the liquid cash on hand for this purpose. My realtor knew how disappointing this was for me and my home-buying experience.

One day, he called me and asked if I had thought about purchasing a newly built home, and if I considered purchasing a house that was a little further south of where I was looking at that time. I never thought of purchasing a newly built home, but due to the current circumstances, I was willing to explore the opportunity. I reiterate this often, *"We may have the plans already set for our lives, but it is God who has the final say."* He wants the absolute best for us, and sometimes His plans for us require us to go through some faith-trialing times, but in the end, we are stronger and more vigilant in trusting Him in all circumstances that we encounter.

Purchasing my first home came with a huge test of my faith as I navigated the process in a country-wide troubling housing market. I had already given my landlord the notice of ending my lease agreement, yet I had not had an active purchase contract on a house. Time was winding down quickly, and I had 30 days left to close on a home. Jeremiah 29: 11 says, *"For I know the plans I have for you,' declares the Lord, 'plans to prosper you and not to harm you, plans to give you hope and a future."* My life is led by this Scripture, and although we read and hear it often, it becomes a testimony as we walk in all that God has for us each day, and when we allow God to have His way in our lives. Trust me, His way is the best because He knows what is around the corner, He knows how to prepare us, and He knows what we will need to prepare for what is to come. I can confidently say that this passage in the Bible is the foundation and fruit of all our lives if we are willing to trust and believe in it. So, allowing God to do His will in our lives will allow us to experience His best in our lives. This is where peace and happiness reside. This is where growth and healing reside. This is where manifestation and purpose reside. This is where we pour out and release the gifts and testimonies that God has blessed us with to share with the world.

We should want to walk in alignment with God because His plan for us will feel just right, and it will allow us to execute at our highest potential and positively impact the world. God's plan will supersede everything else, and it will fall in line with what we were created to do on this earth. So do not avoid it, receive it, be obedient in it, and thrive in it. We can run, but we can't hide from God. Running toward our destiny will not be a feeling of weariness, exhaustion, confusion, hate, jealousy, insecurity, or failure. Walking in our destiny feels like victory, fulfillment, joy, accomplishment, and a testimony that will bless and encourage others to trust God in every area of their life.

My realtor made an appointment with the builder to show me the remainder of the newly built homes that were left in their new subdivision inventory in McDonough. I did not know what to expect, but I was willing to explore an opportunity that I had never intended to take because it had never crossed my mind to go on the new build route. Plus, it just seemed too far out of my reach at this time in my life. However, I had to place the helmet of faith on my head, and when my realtor explained to me the purchase perks offered by the builder, I was quite excited and convinced that this was the route that I needed to take in my first-time home-buying journey. There was something that the realtor said to me that rang a bell in my ears. No down payment and no closing costs. The purchase included a refrigerator, dishwasher, stove, washer, and dryer. ALL stainless-steel appliances were included in the deal, and so it felt like a total win.

Needless to say, I took the leap of faith and signed a contract with the Legacy Home Builder Company at that time. My realtor scheduled an appointment for us to meet with the builder's representative the following week. There were four pre-built homes that were available for me to tour that had previous offers, where the deals had unfortunately fallen through. I prayed over my decision-making process and selected the 2152 square foot single-family, four-bedroom home. The house included a guest bedroom on the main floor and three bedrooms on the second level, vaulted and trayed ceilings on the second floor, one full bath on the main floor, two full baths on the second floor, a two-car garage, and a backyard with a cement patio. On top of all of that, the price was a steal! I was sold on this house! I was excited about finally focusing on one house and preparing for a hassle-free closing experience. I also knew in my heart that this was my *"starter"* home and that my family and I would create the best memories in this house.

My children were super excited about the move and the new home where they would have their own personal space as they began to grow into their pre-teen and teenage years. I was at peace with my decision; I graciously thanked my realtor, and we began the packing and moving process. I was finally going to be a homeowner. My family was very excited and eager to get settled into their own space. Although I was excited to move to my new home, I felt a little nervous because this was my first time owning something this big and being fully responsible for repairs and maintenance now. I was used to calling the landlord or maintenance person to fix any housing repairs. I was always told that it is important to create a household account in these cases so that the funds are available when needed, specifically for this purpose. I was very excited to gain the experience of becoming a homeowner after helping others experience it for years.

After getting settled in our new home, I began to decorate and shop for different home essentials. By this time, I was on a hybrid work-from-home arrangement where I worked. This was perfect. However, I found it quite difficult to pull my children out of such an amazing school district in Gwinnett County. A school district that we all had grown to love and enjoy so much. With that, I drove them to school for almost an hour one way each day. Their father stepped in and put an end to it, enrolling them in their respective schools in our new district while I was at work. I came to accept that the change was good for them; they needed to connect with the children and teachers in the community we now call home.

I realized that in every school environment, parents who are involved and remain informed of their children's work performance, educational, and overall school experience are what matters most. Plus, that was a lot of driving for me every day! My children continued to do well in school academically and socially. So, if they were doing well, I would do well and not worry. My children enjoyed the new school, their new teachers, and made lots of new friends.

My son was a leader and a young trailblazer, and upon entering high school, he became popular for his charisma, handsomeness, wisdom, and confidence. VP Jr. was a good student, and his teachers enjoyed him. He was able to balance schoolwork, participate in sports, and run his own clothing line business named Clubhouse Clothing. VP Jr.'s clothing line was received by many and had a great influence on the young people that he engaged with at school and in the local community. VP Jr.'s work even caught the attention of some celebrity hip-hop music artists who showed their support for his products and mission. VP Jr. also loved music and was included on the hook of one of his dad's song releases, *"100 Racks."* VP Jr. was so great in his craft that he was even offered an investment opportunity for his clothing line. I was such an impressed mama bear!

We were all impressed by VP Jr.'s talent, creativity, and influence. As a proud mother, I was there in every way for my children. VP Jr.'s talent brought young men and women together in peace and harmony, celebrating their love for hip-hop music and hip-hop culture in the community. In addition, balance is the key.

VP Jr. was also the first pick for the 100 Black Men of South Metro Atlanta Mentee program in high school. The mentors who conducted the interview told me that they never had a young man nail the interview the way that VP Jr. did, and he was most definitely selected. What a wonderful organization and program that mentored young men of color and focused on the importance of education, community, and scholarship, being well-traveled, well-spoken, to have etiquette and respect in all that they do. The young men also created their own pitches and elevator speeches. I was thoroughly impressed and supported my son in every way while he was a student in this respectable program.

VV was on the quiet and shy side like me and so when she decided to sign up for anything, I had to assure that she completed the full cycle and stuck with it whether it was cheerleading, basketball, and JROTC program in high school that she was accidentally enrolled in but was encouraged to remain in the class and ended up enjoying the program and her instructor. She received a lot out of this program, and this is what it is all about: finishing with growth and a positive experience. My children had adjusted well to our new community, and that was one less concern for me. Thank God!

Proverbs 20:7 says, *"Fathers, do not exasperate your children; instead, bring them up in the training and instruction of the Lord."* I made every effort and decision pertaining to my children with the mindset of seeking God first in the process, in my actions toward others, and in choosing the way of the Lord in how I walked in my life, praying that they will exemplify this when they became adults and parents one day. As we continued to move forward with life in Georgia, we enjoyed each other even more. We created memories every day and also went on family vacations to visit loved ones in New York, nearby Disney amusement parks in Orlando, Florida, and beaches in nearby Myrtle Beach, North Carolina, Savannah, Georgia, and Hilton Head, South Carolina, to name a few.

We very much valued vacation time each year, and soon after we relocated, my children enjoyed their summer breaks from school and the opportunity to spend time in New York with family and friends. This arrangement helped to maintain balance in their lives as well as mine. While they were with family for the summer, I was able to enjoy time to myself and enjoy some fantastic self-care, traveling, and happy moments with my sister-friends and coworkers. In fact, I experienced Essence Fest for the very first time after relocating to Georgia while my kids were in New York for the summer.

A group of my sister-friends and I traveled to New Orleans, and we had a great time. My first time attending was more than an amazing experience. I really enjoyed the New Orleans vibe and culture, the savory food, the cultural music, and the richly historical artwork that displayed the city's story and roots. I always read Essence magazines, which was my favorite, and I regularly subscribed to them, but to walk in its unique style and culture in the streets of New Orleans at Essence Fest was simply the best and very much phenomenal. I was thoroughly impressed as a first timer, and I planned to attend again! Essence is known to educate Black women and the Black community in many facets of life, ranging from health and beauty, accolades for milestones in the Black community, news and events, entertainment, and fashion. Essence remains a cornerstone for women of color and the Black community, and I am all for its purpose and what it represents and means to us all as a people.

I strongly feel that the Black woman, in her strength and resilience, lays the foundation for the community and is the vice that holds every aspect of the Black community together as we do what we do each day in a multi-dimensional way. There are several hats worn by Black women, and our work is never done. We are the mothers of the earth, and the virtuous spirit in us reigns as strength and resilience that comes from our God. We were created to birth not only children but also the foundation on which others can thrive. We are powerful, thus making our children, husbands, families, and communities powerful. When we are powerful, our impact as we walk in our purpose is powerful. With this, I prioritize self-care, self-awareness, family and friends, peace, love, happiness, and most importantly, my relationship with God. These are the key values needed to carry out our purpose unapologetically.

My kids had a very active social life, so I was also that soccer mom who transported my kids and friends in my eight-seater, GMC Acadia SUV at the time, from point A to Z on any given day. As my children began to mature, they developed a desire to obtain their driver's license. I was super nervous about this, but at some point, we have to allow our eagles to fly. So, with practice, VP Jr. decided to take his driver's test, and he passed. Two years later, VV also took her driver's license test and passed. I was very happy for them as this was a strong form of independence for them. It was also great for me as I sometimes needed them to run quick errands for me at times. I think most of us parents were happy to be able to call on our newly licensed children to stop at the grocery store to grab some milk or eggs so that we can finish making dinner or breakfast. I was one of them.

I was still a little nervous because my babies were now driving on the same roads as those who may not drive as safely as they should. So, being the praying mother that I am, I prayed whenever my kiddos hit the road on their own. Oftentimes, my kids drove together when they left the house. I loved that because if they were out anywhere together, they knew to keep a close eye out for each other, no matter what. This gave me comfort knowing that my kids had each other's backs at the end of the day. They were raised to be this way.

VP worked on his security business and his music. In my downtime, he would invite me to visit him at his music studio to hang out, go to lunch, or to simply listen to his newest track or sound. It is true that the apple does not fall far from the tree, because I had noticed how his sons seemed to walk in his footsteps in music.

One day, while I was in the office, I received a call on my cell phone from the local ambulance. I was informed that VP had been shot multiple times while at his music studio and that they were rushing him to the local trauma hospital. Worried sick, I told my boss and colleagues that I had to leave and would contact them as soon as I could.

As I rushed to the hospital, my mind was all over the place. I was nervous and full of worry. Once I arrived at the hospital, I sat in the waiting room for what seemed like years, as I waited to hear back from the hospital surgeons. As I waited, I made calls to VP's sister, who lived in Georgia, and my mother, who lived in New York. I did not want my children to know just yet, as I was still waiting for the status of VP's condition. Whenever I asked for a status, the response was that they were still working on him. I continued to wait as other loved ones and friends arrived. We all waited together, and while in the waiting room, the six o'clock evening news came on, and it reported the incident. This was a day full of emotions, worries, and heavy praying.

Finally, after several hours had passed, the doctors called us in to provide an update on VP's condition. We were so thankful and appreciative of the hospital surgeons. I thanked God for His hand in this process! I thank God for Grady Hospital and its trauma medical staff. Sometime later, other family and friends arrived. Our two children told me that they had learned about the incident when someone informed them after watching the news that evening.

My son, VP Jr., fell to his knees when he walked in and saw his father lying in a hospital bed with all the machines, tubes, and bandages all over him. Seeing his dad in this way broke him. I felt so bad and wanted to immediately soothe the pain for all his children. We spent time with VP in the hospital that evening after he was deemed stable and ready to begin the road to recovery. God is the guide, protector, and healer of His sheep. He extends to us His grace and favor often and in many ways, even when we do not realize it. God is always watching and covering us in our daily movements. Without God, I am nothing!

Second Samuel 22:38 says, *"And David spake unto the Lord the words of this song in the day that the Lord had delivered him out of the hand of all his enemies, and out of the hand of Saul: And he said, The Lord is my rock and my fortress and my deliverer."* God has the power to shift any situation that we may face. We must trust that the moving of His hand has a lot to do with our faith and the ability to lay our requests at His feet and leave them there, trusting that He can make a way out of no way. We should not continue to go back to the concern or struggle with what could possibly happen if the concern is not addressed by our God within the timeframe that we expect it to be. We must leave it at God's feet and continually trust Him as we wait.

As my children and I left the hospital, we left with a spirit of gratitude and thankfulness that God protected their father that day. We were at peace knowing that God had us covered in His love and care and that He is able in ALL situations, including this one. While the process had some rough patches, God smoothed them out. VP had a host of loved ones and friends visiting him in the hospital while he was there, and I am sure that this was a huge encouragement in his healing process. My children and I focused on making sure their father was doing well and fully supported in his healing journey. The outpouring of love that VP received at that difficult time was a gift from God, and we thanked God for His grace and mercy every day in all things.

As time progressed, VP was released from the hospital and advanced successfully on the road to recovery. God is amazing! His children were happy and excited about their father's improved condition. As VP walked in his path to recovery, he continued to do what he enjoyed, which was making music. We all enjoyed listening to his music and watching his performances as he navigated the healing process. The detectives handling the case interviewed VP multiple times and provided updates regularly. A couple of months later, the police were able to make arrests of the individuals who were involved in the shooting. When the police revealed who they were, we were unaware of who they were. However, it was great to obtain closure on the case and to ensure that appropriate measures had been taken against the guilty party.

Although VP was physically separated and lived in a different state, a formal divorce was necessary and was the appropriate way things needed to be handled. He continued to explain to me that the other party refused to agree. He explained to me that he had initiated discussions to complete the process. He shared that he continued to try without success. One day, his estranged wife traveled to Georgia to see him at the hospital, where he was receiving outpatient care after the incident. Unexpectedly, the three of us were in the exam room together waiting for his doctor to enter, and I did not see it coming when he brought up divorce discussions with her while in my presence. It happened so fast. The space felt awkward and uncomfortable. I wanted to slip out of the room and leave for them to discuss in private. But there was no response from her in return, and then the doctor entered. However, I did not wish to be in the midst of that discussion. The space felt totally uncomfortable.

As time went on, VP continued to progress in his craft as he recovered. His healing journey required us all to assist with an all-hands-on-deck approach, and we did just that. There were some rough patches at times because there were some frustrations due to his current condition and being immobile for months. The situation and recovery were very much life-changing and weighed very heavily on all of us on some days. I truly loved him, and I knew in my heart without a doubt that he felt the same way. One of his aunts, whom he was close to, had previously shared with me his feelings about me that he discussed with her and his desires for our future. I felt the same way as we had a long journey of love, children, ups and downs, separation, joy, frustration, etc. The love we shared ran over a long period of time, almost two decades. Ultimately, VP and I ended up parting ways almost a year after the incident for reasons that did not align with the paths we had for ourselves and the path that God had for us.

I prayed for resolution and peace in every area of my life and his life. I prayed over every situation surrounding me, and I asked God for forgiveness in all areas of my life where I may have done wrong knowingly and unknowingly. Psalm 51:1 says, *"Have mercy on me, O God, according to your steadfast love; according to your abundant mercy blot out my transgressions."* My heart and intentions remained pure and always will. I continued to pray for this.

The kids and I had not heard from their dad much after the shift in our circumstances. It was a very difficult process for everyone, but I am sure that he knew how much he was loved by us, despite everything else. My children adored their father, and he adored them. Their bond with him was priceless, and it remained priceless.

CHAPTER

Seven

New Encounters, Spiritual Growth, and Divine Direction

One evening after months of focusing on myself, I decided to get out of the house and enjoy some time outdoors, knowing that this too is a part of self-care. As I stepped out for some *"ME"* time and to enjoy some girl time with two of my close friends, B and M, whom I met when I first moved to Georgia at the company where I worked, four years prior. We went to an outdoor concert to see Jaheim, Kem, and Anthony Hamilton at Chastain Park Amphitheatre in Atlanta. The show was awesome, and when it was over, my friends and I were making our way to our vehicles when we met a gentleman named CN who stepped off the tour bus and introduced himself to us. He was friendly and respectful to us ladies, and he and I later exchanged numbers and kept in touch.

He lived in Detroit, and whenever he came to town, he and I hung out and enjoyed time together. He was nothing less than a gentleman, and I can tell that he was raised right, always displaying love and respect. We remained in touch by talking on the phone regularly and Skyping when he was not in town for a show or to visit. I loved that he planned out the location of the date before we connected for the day or evening. We dated off and on for about a year. As much as I felt that CN was a wonderful catch, I feel that it was the long distance and his being on the road for work often. He worked in the music industry. His job was awesome, but it was a concern for me as he was away from home often.

CN never gave me a direct reason not to trust him. However, I realized that dating someone who works in this capacity may be challenging when it comes to time and family life. Of course, I respected his career and wanted him to continue to flourish in what he did best in his expertise, and what he had been called to do. Eventually, we regretfully parted ways. So, for almost a year, I was focusing on myself and my spiritual growth, which also included navigating through the fellowship experience at churches in the area where we resided. I visited different churches in my area, and I began to narrow down what I liked most and what I did not prefer in the process. Some churches I visited more often than others, and some I chose not to return to in the future for a reason or two. I realized that I prefer smaller churches, but not too small. So, as we visited, we learned and experienced different churches with different practices until we figured out where God drew us to as a permanent church home. This took some time as the church home selection process required many aspects to consider for myself and my children.

There was one church in McDonough, WC UMC, that we visited for a long period of time, and we enjoyed every aspect of the church. The leaders of this church were of God's work, and their messages from God resonated with me every Sunday. The messages groomed me and nurtured my spirit. The messages were authentic and backed up with powerful scriptures and testimonies. Our pastor spoke to us about our daily walk with God. He spoke about aligning with God's will for our lives and the importance of maintaining the right walk and talk in word and in our actions.

I found it to be funny, yet so true, when he spoke to women who had an interest in getting married one day. When the pastor addressed this group, the pastor mentioned that when praying to God for a husband, a woman will need to be specific because women of God don't want just any man. He said that if you want your future husband to be a man of God, ask God, if you want him to be hard-working, speak it to God with a request, if you want him to be handsome, ask God about it, if you want him to be smart, talk to God, and if a woman wants her future husband to be a provider, ask for God's blessings in his ability to provide. The sermon delivery of the pastor, Pastor TR, was hilarious at times but very true, and so I included this way of organizing my thoughts in every area of my prayer life. Reading the Bible continues to be the blueprint for me as I maneuver through life and in every aspect of my life.

Pastor TR was straightforward and to the point with his messages, and all we could do was laugh and respect them. I highly respect authenticity. We continued to attend Sunday service there for all it offered us in spirit and in truth of God's word. We learned and participated in serving God and His people. This church also had a great youth program.

Nearly a year or so after CN and I severed ties, I decided to join some friends at a New Year's Eve party at another friend's home. The party was held in their finished basement, which was gorgeous with a dance floor and a wraparound bar for entertainment purposes. The party was amazing, and my friends and I were dancing on the dance floor and enjoyed every minute of the old school hip-hop, reggae, and R&B. The following Friday, the same friends and I went to our usual Happy Hour hole-in-the-wall spot on Old National Highway, called the PB. We absolutely loved this place! I always brought all my out-of-town guests to this place when they visited, and they always enjoyed everything about it.

The PB had the best bucket of crab legs for $10 and $3 *"happy hour"* drink specials in town. You can take $20 with you to this place, and still have a great time there on a Friday evening. This was a great place to go after a long week of working hard, and sometimes my coworkers and I would go to unwind after a long and busy work week.

It was the first week of 2012. I was 38 years old, and I was looking forward to something different and something NEW in the new year.

There was a large group of us that evening, and most of my friends were chatting with each other at the bar. There must have been almost ten of us in tow that evening, enjoying an early New Year's weekend of conversations, music, cocktails, and dancing. As the place began to get packed, I started to move closer to where my friends were sitting near the bar so that I could remain in the loop. As I leaned on one of the poles at the center of the platform where the bar was located, I listened to our favorite DJ spin the tracks. I looked over and saw one of my friends talking to two gentlemen as they walked inside the venue. Before I knew it, she walked over to me with one of the men, introducing him to me.

He said his name was LS, and I told him mine. He formally introduced himself to me and explained what he did for a living and what he was in the process of aspiring to do. I, of course, did the same. I was very impressed with him and his long list of accomplishments and endeavors, and he was impressed with me and my career and life attributes. He told me that he had two children, a son and a daughter, and I told him that I also had two children, a son and a daughter. His children were in their early 20s, with one in college and playing college basketball, and the other who recently completed college and was successfully managing her own business. My children were teens in high school and were active in different programs and sports. I told him my age, and I tried to guess his age, but I was far off. I thought that he was younger than me; however, he was four years older than me. He looked much younger than he was, which is always a good thing. Our conversation was mesmerizing, and so we talked the entire time that we were there. The eye contact and chemistry were amazing, and I was in awe of his demeanor and handsomeness, how he was dressed, his accomplishments, and his intelligence.

He had earned two master's degrees, while I had a bachelor's degree at the time, though I hoped to pursue my master's when the timing was right. As we talked, he shared that his cousin had originally planned to go straight to another lounge down the road that evening, but decided to stop by the PB to check out the scene, and ended up staying after meeting us. It felt like divine timing.

About an hour later, our group decided to move on to another spot on the strip called Backstage, a place known for the *"grown and sexy"* crowd, mature, fun-loving, and stylish. As I stepped outside to my car, I saw LS and his cousin slowly driving around the parking lot in his new Mercedes-Benz, which he later said he had gifted himself after retiring from the military.

When I got into my SUV and started it, I looked back and noticed LS had gently blocked me in. He got out and walked over to my driver's side. I stepped out, and he asked for my phone number. I told him we were all heading to the same place, and I would share it when we got there since the others had already left and we were running behind. He said he asked me at that time, just in case we got separated or missed each other later, and he did not want to miss the chance. I felt the same, so we exchanged numbers before heading out.

When I arrived at the next venue, I saw LS, his cousin, and my friends already settled in, and they had brought cocktails for everyone. LS then suggested that he and I move to a more quiet area so that we could hear each other better over the music. He wanted us to get to know each other more, and I was completely open to it.

We sat together, talked, laughed, and danced the night away. I had never felt that kind of connection so quickly with someone before; it was unfamiliar, intense, and beautiful all at once. While we talked, I found myself watching him closely, feeling deeply moved by the moment. I couldn't explain it, but I felt a strong sense that our meeting was meant to be.

While we danced, the song *"Cause I Love You"* by Lenny Williams came on, and LS sang it to me like we had known each other for years. I felt seen and special in that moment.

Later, back at our seats, LS spoke about his family, especially his mother, and how hard she worked to raise them. I had never heard someone speak so highly and so passionately about their family. That alone drew me closer to him.

He was captivating inside and out, grounded, expressive, and full of warmth. We shared a natural chemistry, on and off the dance floor, and everything about that night felt unforgettable.

The feeling was powerful. As we continued to talk, we learned that we are both under the Taurus the Bull zodiac sign and our birthdays are exactly two weeks apart. We were all smiles and wanted to spend more time together again soon. As the night began to wind down, we all prepared to leave the venue. LS drove three of my friends and me to my SUV because we had to park farther away from the venue, as the parking lot was completely full when we arrived. He was such a gentleman.

This was one of the best nights of my life. I had a deep feeling that LS was going to be someone that will be especially important in my life. We all eventually left to go home for the evening. LS and I continued to remain in touch with each other. He told me that he was interested in starting a new career as a civilian employee in Georgia or in the surrounding area. He was very diligent in his new job search efforts, and he asked if I would visit him wherever he landed his next job. Of course, I said yes.

Meanwhile, I continued to work in my career as a managed care contract negotiator in the healthcare industry, and we both took our careers and families seriously and continued to make them a priority. LS and I remained connected and hung out in our town south of the Metro Atlanta area often. His cooking was amazing, and that really impressed me. He told me that his mother was a retired cook for a hotel chain, and she taught him how to cook when he was young. He told me that his mother told him that if a man wants to eat, he needs to know how to cook. I have so much appreciation for mothers like that. The next couple of months were like a summer breeze, warm, soft, and flowing smoothly as we spent time together and got more acquainted. That summer, we even revisited and re-enacted our first meeting at the two venues the night that we first met, and we danced the night away everywhere we went.

One night at a comedy club, we danced so long that we closed the place down. We were literally the very last two to leave as they were turning the lights out. Although it had only been months since I had met LS, I felt a deep connection with him quickly, as if we had known each other for several years already. I recall regularly listening to the local R&B radio station during the spring and summer of 2012, which just so happened to always be the *"bomb."*

One of my favorite songs by one of my favorite music artists was in heavy rotation at that time. The song and artist were *"Don't Mind"* by Mary J. Blige, and I found it to be very strange that whenever the song played on the radio, LS popped up in my mind every single time. It felt as if it were me talking to him in the song. But I wondered why, because this was such a new connection. Was God communicating something to me about LS that soon after we met? Was this song a prophecy for what was to come for LS and me? Those same words had yet to be spoken to him by me, but every time I heard them, I was consumed with thoughts of him. I was not sure why this was happening, but God works in mysterious ways. God works ahead of us. God tends to drop signs and hints of what is to come. Although there are times when situations do not make sense to us in the present, God shows us the reasons why later.

Although LS and I had recently met, our connection was strong, and we shared a lot in common. He shared a lot of personal information with me, and I did the same with him. We learned that we had very similar likes and dislikes. Perhaps he was my soul mate, and this is why everything felt so light, easy, and intriguing for both of us. If there was such a thing as love at first sight, I would name our first meeting as such. The feeling could not be described. All I knew was that it just felt perfect. He also voiced to me the same sentiment regarding our first meeting.

As time passed after submitting applications, LS began to hear back from recruiters. He was offered a position out of state that he accepted. After he informed me of the good news, I was very happy for him. He wanted us to remain in contact with each other, and he asked me if I was planning to visit him out of state after he relocated. The answer was yes and yes for sure. At this point, I felt that we had fallen for each other. I began to get sad because I did not understand why God allowed me to cross paths with LS, spend seven months getting to know him and enjoying time with him, just for us to be separated by states. Although it was a very difficult process, I knew that he had to do what he had to do for himself and for his family. I was very proud of him!

One day, while we were talking on the phone before he relocated, he asked me how I would feel about my name being changed (he wanted me to take his last name with mine). I began to blush inside, smiling with a very full, happy heart, saying yes, I would love it. I wanted the same as him. I loved the thought of being his wife and wondered how amazing it would be. LS was married some years before to his children's mother and had been divorced for quite some time. I had not been married yet, but felt that the time was right, and I was ready and prepared in every way: mentally, emotionally, and now spiritually.

So, as the last couple of days were wrapping up for us to spend time together in Georgia before he officially relocated, I went over to his place, and one of his cousins, JB, who was like a brother to him, was there. We both were helping LS pack up the rest of his belongings, and I folded laundry. I ended up staying overnight, and LS cooked a delicious breakfast for us the next morning. I especially enjoyed the homemade hashbrowns that he made from freshly cut potatoes with onions and peppers. Goodness gracious, all I can say is yum!

JB always had me laughing. He and I liked *"poking fun"* at each other and cracking jokes, so we did just that on that day. As reality set in, I had to face the fact that LS was moving away to another state. I knew that he did his best to find an open position in the Atlanta area before resorting to a nearby state. Atlanta was, of course, his first choice to work and live. I felt that our hearts would remain connected no matter what.

Although the distance was not far, he was not here in Georgia with me. In the book of Romans 8:28, it says, *"And we know that in all things God works for the good of those who love Him, who have been called according to his purpose."* I believe that there was a significant purpose in our initial meeting and the time spent together. God introduced us in His Divine timing and allowed us this special time of connection for a reason, although he was now moving away. The purpose I did not know at the time, but I know that God makes no mistakes, and any of the time spent together between the two of us did not go to waste. LS's spirit and wisdom filled my spirit with the peace that gave me everything that I needed to carry me through the distance between us, living in two different towns.

He traveled to Georgia regularly, and he excelled in his career, and I did the same in my career. We often supported each other in the work that we did. I decided to obtain my certification in project management at a nearby college, and this assisted me in managing my workload in my current role and prepared me for future project management assignments and roles.

I loved how LS would keep me in the loop of his accolades and accomplishments, which were a lot. He made me so proud. I made him proud. He was blessed to travel the world, not just in the military but also in his new position, where he oversaw global contracts that he completed and managed. I was excited to see the wonderful pictures and videos that he had taken in various places that he traveled to across the world to meet the leaders who handled the international accounts that he negotiated. I was greatly inspired and in awe by such a wonderful blessing that God had bestowed on him. LS was such a blessing to my soul. The distinctive way that my pastor taught us to pray when making requests must have been successful at making their way to God because it seems as if God was beginning to deliver them to me.

As time went by and LS and I became closer, we spoke about plans for when he retired and moved back to Georgia. I always looked forward to his visits in the interim. My children really liked him, and when my grandson Josiah was born, LS immediately assumed the role of grandfather to him, and my grandson adored him. My children respected him and developed a positive and caring relationship with him. It is interesting that whenever any of us were in a moment of overwhelm, we would call LS. He was always prepared to listen, console, guide, and find a resolution to anything concerning us. He had a steady calmness about him that gave us insight when we were stressed and gave us peace when we were overwhelmed with whatever had transpired in that hour. We were always thankful for LS and his presence in our lives.

My favorite thing about him is how he always shared the Word of God in some form with me whenever we spent time together. I prayed for a man who feared God. Even though LS was in a position where he had to relocate for his job, it seemed to be for a specific purpose, as if God used it to build something up in both of us. Was it to build character and faith in what He had spoken to us the first day LS and I met?

I continued to move forward in faith, praying over the situation, leaving it with God. We continued to hang out together as time permitted. He made many attempts to transfer to Georgia for work, but there were not many open positions in this very popular area, and when he did find one, his daily one-way commute would have been way too far out of the area. He was trying very hard to relocate to Georgia. Georgia was where he was born and raised, and most of his family lived here. Perhaps this was all a part of how God planned it.

A couple of years after LS and I met, he began to have the baby *"itch"* that came with the desire to have a child with me. He asked me about us having a baby, and I told him that if we have a child at this stage in life, we will be Abraham and Sarah in the book of Genesis of the Holy Bible. He laughed. I laughed. We moved forward with the mindset that if God chooses to bless us with one, then this is how we will receive it, as a blessing. A miracle. Psalm 77:14 says, *"You are the God who performs miracles; you display your power among the peoples."* My doctor had previously informed me at my annual checkup that my chances for pregnancy were slim and at less than ten percent due to my uterine fibroids. So with that, we left our desires at the feet of God.

One weekend when LS was in town, he made the family a seafood feast. It was delicious, and our bellies were so full and content afterward. After he left the house, I had not heard back from him that evening, and so I tried calling him. He seemed to be slow to answer his phone and to return my calls after he had left the house. It felt like something was a little off and not typical of him. I became a bit frustrated, and when we finally talked, he mentioned that he was dealing with something *"deep,"* and then he said, *"But I know for sure that I love you."* Of course, I felt the same way about him, and I prayed over the matter because I was not sure exactly what was going on with him. However, I continued to think positively in hopes that whatever the issue, God will help him through it, that God will help us through it.

Habakkuk 2:3, *"For still the vision awaits its appointed time; it hastens to the end-it will not lie. If it seems slow, wait for it; it will surely come; it will not delay."* As difficult as it was, I had to learn to embrace patience and understanding because when something is meant to be, it will be, because God is the one who is in complete control, and I only want for me what God wants for me. That is it, and that is all.

CHAPTER

Eight

Navigating Life in the Midst of Tragedy, Pain, and Difficulty

VP and I had been apart for almost two years, and the kids and I had not heard from him in quite a bit of time. We learned that he had recently moved from Atlanta to Connecticut some months prior. The last time I had spoken to him was about six months or so before hearing about him moving away. The call was about keeping an eye on our children's social media activity and watching over his baby girl, VV. Fathers are super overprotective of their girls, and VP was just that. I did not have a social media account at that time; however, I had my people watchers who specifically watched my children's behavior while on social media and kept up with my children when they were online.

Of course, their father was one of the watchers too, the main watcher. Not very long after hearing that VP had moved to Connecticut, my daughter received a call from her aunt, informing her that her father had been critically shot and had multiple fatal wounds. My daughter was told that her father was in critical condition. We were all a mess, but we were really hopeful and prayed heavily. He wasn't doing well, and his sister was at the hospital in Connecticut and allowed VP Jr. and VV to talk to their father on her phone because he could hear them but was unable to talk. As they talked to him, she told us that tears rolled down his face. My God, this hurt so bad!

A week later, VP succumbed to his injuries. Our hearts were broken, crushed! My son, VP Jr., disappeared for hours when he heard about the passing of his father, as he was not home when he was informed by someone else. We were all so upset, and I did not know where my son was in this very difficult hour, so I was afraid. His 100 Black Men mentor finally located him and brought him home. We all cried together. How do you console two grieving children at one time while trying to keep yourself contained?

This was one of the most difficult obstacles that I ever had to face. Their pain was my pain, and I had my own separate pain. I immediately began planning for us to head up to New York. I requested time off from work, and I rented a car so that my children and I could drive up to New York for their father's funeral service and to be with family. My kids absolutely adored their father, and to experience loss in this way was beyond devastating. While on the road, LS called to check on us and to see if we were okay and if we needed anything. I told him that we were doing okay and thanked him for checking on us.

After nearly 15 hours of driving, we finally arrived home in New York. Surrounded by loved ones, we comforted one another. My family and VP's family prepared food for the repast, and I was deeply grateful for how everyone came together when we needed it most. We prayed, showed love, and supported each other, though I was still in disbelief. I had to stay strong because my children needed me more than ever.

This tragedy changed our lives forever. My children, just 15 and 17, now had to face life without their father, a young man who had just turned 40 the month before. What happened to him was senseless, rooted in evil and hate. As it says in the Bible, in Romans 12:19, *"Beloved, do not avenge yourselves… 'Vengeance is Mine, I will repay,' says the Lord."* I trusted that justice would come in God's time.

VP's service was deeply emotional. His best friend and cousin, JH, delivered a powerful eulogy. Having known VP almost his entire life, he honored him in the most fitting way. At the burial, the weather was calm and sunny until the final words were spoken. As we said our last goodbyes, a sudden, heavy downpour came from every direction. In that moment, it felt like VP's sorrow was pouring over us all. I will never forget it.

My first love, my children's father, and one of my greatest supporters, who always believed I could do anything, was gone. It didn't feel real.

I knew the road ahead for us would be incredibly hard. The three of us had to hold each other closer than ever, leaning on love as we navigated our new reality.

While in New York, my children spent time with their siblings and loved ones, finding comfort in those bonds. After two days, we returned to Georgia and gave ourselves grace as we adjusted to life again.

I was especially thankful that their high school offered a support group for students who had lost a parent. My children joined and discovered classmates who shared similar losses. That space gave them connection, understanding, and a sense of peace. I also sought counseling through my job, church, and close circle, and we attended sessions together as a family.

It was very helpful because we truly needed it. Grieving became a daily process, and through prayer and our close relationship with God, my children and I were sustained, and we still are today.

After losing VP, I felt God nudging me to finally join the church I had been visiting for years. It was time to commit. My daughter and I joined together, making church a firm part of our foundation. Obedience to God is everything to me. As *Deuteronomy 28:1* reminds us, *"If you fully obey the Lord your God… He will set you high above all the nations."* I choose obedience, always.

As VP Jr. entered his senior year, life became busy with deadlines, activities, sports, and his clothing brand. I made sure he stayed on track with graduation and college requirements, entrance exams, applications, prom plans, and more. He handled it all well and chose Valdosta State University, about three hours from home. Close enough for me to check in, lol! I was a proud mama.

Graduation was unforgettable. Family came from New York and the Carolinas, and friends showed up strong. The ceremony was outdoors, and our cheers for VP Jr. filled the entire field. He also received a scholarship from 100 Black Men of South Metro Atlanta. We celebrated with an epic party. My son truly had the *"IT"* factor: a leader, a protector, and a trendsetter. I've always been honored to be his mother.

A few weeks later, we moved him into his dorm. The campus was beautiful and welcoming. After settling him in, we grabbed food and headed home. I believed he would do well, though I had some concerns about distractions, especially since his girlfriend had moved nearby. She was a good young woman, but I still hoped he would stay focused.

Thankfully, his first year went smoothly. He chose to major in Communications, a perfect fit for his personality, his love for music, and his natural ability to connect with people. Communications was the right path for him.

I remained hopeful and encouraging toward my son, knowing this was a major step toward his bright future.

Just a month before VP Jr.'s graduation, we celebrated VV's sweet 16 after such a difficult year losing her father. The theme was *"Tiffany and Company,"* with everything in Tiffany Blue, even her signature punch. Some food was catered, and the rest was lovingly prepared by family and friends. Her custom cake was beautifully made by a nurse from my job who owns a baking business.

I gifted VV her first *"Tiffany and Company"* necklace, along with outfits and special trinkets. Her makeup was done at Sephora, and we finally found her Tiffany Blue dress at Dillard's in Dunwoody at Perimeter Mall. A coworker and her husband designed stunning invitations and custom water bottles with VV's photo, and with help from friends, the venue was decorated beautifully.

We closely chaperoned a large group of teens as they ate, danced, and enjoyed the night. The same person who handled VP Jr.'s senior prom photoshoot also captured VV's special day. It was refreshing to see the teens interact with respect and joy, no drama, just genuine fun and lasting memories.

Hosting two milestone celebrations back-to-back in April and May was exhausting, but I'm grateful for the love and support that carried us through.

A mother's love always rises to meet her children's needs. They are her reason and her driving force. As *Isaiah 66:13* says, *"As one whom his mother comforts, so will I comfort you."* That comfort reflects God's love flowing through us. From pregnancy to delivery, one of life's most vulnerable and powerful experiences, motherhood begins with sacrifice and continues with purpose.

God entrusts women with the gift of bringing life into the world, and I am deeply honored to be VP Jr.'s and VV's mother. I have never taken this role lightly. My children are my gifts from God, and every decision I make is rooted in what's best for them. As *Proverbs 1:8-9* reminds us, a mother's guidance is a lasting blessing that shapes her children's lives forever.

CHAPTER

Nine

Regroup, Reprioritize, and Receive Love and Guidance from God

After a couple of months of VP Jr. being away at college, I received a call from the administrator advising me that he had been up every night for the last couple of nights and not sleeping or eating. He was also not attending his classes. When I received the call, I was at a local hospital with a friend who needed me to take her there for surgery early that morning. At the time I received the call, she had just completed surgery, and she had awakened from the anesthesia they had given her. Her surgery was a success. My friend was able to arrange for someone else to take her home from the hospital, and I quickly headed on the highway. I had to drive to Valdosta to check on my son.

It was a three-hour drive, and at that moment, I did not know what to think. I was worried, and my mind was on overdrive. I am a praying mother, and so that was what I did. I prayed. When I arrived at the VSU campus, VP Jr. seemed to have been ready to leave. He seemed a little tired and worn out. I felt so bad because he was not himself. I packed up some of his belongings, and we drove home. He fell asleep as soon as we got in the car and slept the entire ride home, and so I just let him rest. This was more than likely the first time in several days that he had been able to have a sound sleep. It obviously was a much-needed sleep.

Once we finally got home, we both went to our bedrooms and fell asleep. The next day we talked, and I wanted him to know that he could talk to me, his *"mama bear,"* about ANYTHING, no matter what. He did not have a lot to say, but I was very observant of him over the past couple of days. He would sleep but not much. I decided to take him to his doctor. The doctor confirmed that he was physically healthy, but will refer us to a mental health therapist. I was happy to know that he was physically healthy, as we were able to rule out anything pertaining to that. So, I checked to see which therapists were in our network that would be the best fit for my son's needs. We met a few providers and eventually chose one that seemed to be more in tune with me, my son, and the best steps to take in getting him back on track.

VP Jr. was diagnosed with a mental health condition that could have been triggered by a major life-changing event. VP Jr. lost his dad the previous year, and of course, it was very traumatic for him. After VP passed, VP Jr. was often told by other people that he had to be strong for his sister and me. That is a heavy weight for anyone, especially a young teen who was still learning and growing in everything as it pertained to life. I was an adult and was still trying to put the pieces together and trying to wrap my head around everything that had transpired over the past year.

Of course, I consulted with God on the next steps regarding a plan for my son. God says in Proverbs 3:5-6, *"Trust in the Lord with all your heart and lean not on your own understanding; in all your ways submit to him, and he will make your paths straight."* I can truly attest to this biblical passage as I have experienced having an interest in doing one thing, and God changed my plan to His plan with a completely different direction because He knows what is best in our lives. God's plans will always prevail, and His plans will always have a purpose for our greater good and for the greater good of others. When we walk in our purpose, God's will for our lives will happen, and when we walk in God's will for our lives, we are walking in peace and fulfillment. God covers us, and when He covers us, we are at our best and glorifying Him at the same time.

God provided me with the strength and the strong will in my spirit to advocate for my son, as it took quite some time, lots of research, and some trial-and-error in concluding the overall matter at hand with an accurate diagnosis, treatment plan, and an ultimate resolution for his care. As a mom, I was always there with and for my son in this process. I was his mom, but I was also his voice and his advocate.

I studied the condition frequently and met with different providers to determine what was best suited for his needs. The process was a long road, but once a solid plan of action with the right providers was put in place, my son was eventually able to navigate in fullness and in harmony with his overall health and wellness.

Mental health is just as important as physical health. For individuals who have experienced a mental health condition or have a loved one who has and may currently be experiencing the impact of a mental health condition or crisis, there is a light at the end of the tunnel. On Pinterest, there is a quote that reads *"Perhaps the butterfly is proof that you can go through a great deal of darkness and still become a butterfly."* This sums it up. There may be dark days that we will encounter in life, but as long as we keep going, we will be able to experience the light that awaits us at the end of the tunnel. The light is equivalent to peace, healing, growth, joy, hope, and all that offers a place of movement in a positive direction. Let us choose to call on God as often as possible, in the good and in the bad.

During this time in my life, I found myself calling on Him day in and day out during the exhaustion, confusion, and despair. I talked to God daily for strength, and I also talked to LS for support in times when I needed encouragement and upliftment from him. In the difficult time in navigating my son's mental health, I became very stressed, and one day I became upset and was crying about my son's situation. LS spoke to me about the story of Lazarus. He mentioned how broken Lazarus's family was when he died and how they pleaded to Jesus for him to be returned to life as soon as possible. But Jesus came when the time was right, and that was when he raised Lazarus from the dead. After listening to LS, my faith in this situation strengthened, and I was refueled in my time of weakness. I thank God for using LS to speak truth and life into me during difficult moments. My son, like Lazarus, rose above his condition. Jesus heard my cry and provided us with relief, healing, peace, and restoration.

Not long after, my daughter gave birth to a beautiful baby boy named Josiah. I was quietly praying that my daughter would give my grandson a biblical name. That meant so much to me. So, I was very happy about this name when she shared it with us! Josiah was a good king in the Bible, and we would all groom him in such an honorable way. Second Chronicles 34:1-25 says, *"Josiah was eight years old when he began to reign in Jerusalem, and he did what was right in the sight of the Lord and walked in the ways of David, his father, and declined neither to the right hand, nor to the left."*

Due to VV's pregnancy and delivery date, she had to complete some of her remaining senior year classes online and virtually through a local private school. She put in the work and graduated from her home school, Dutchtown High School in Henry County. Her godmother, Aunt N, her godsister, TY, and her husband surprised VV with their attendance from South Carolina at her graduation in Georgia. We were all proud of her for continuing to press forward in obtaining her high school diploma. Receiving her high school diploma opened opportunities to create a stable life for herself and her child, my grandchild.

With God's guidance and the work of the holy spirit within us, we can witness our children blossom into the best version of themselves, walking in the purpose God has for them. My goal is to leave a legacy for my children and grandchildren that upholds the importance of leading their own families with God and the Holy Spirit as the internal compass and the captain of their ship in every way. Pouring this into my children and grandchildren is the key action point that will guide them to the unique purpose that they have been born to walk in, within God's perfect timing. I hope that the same faith mindset carries over as they parent their own children.

Parenting isn't about us; it's about the responsibility God entrusts to us. We are called to care for His children not only by bringing them into the world, but by nurturing them emotionally and spiritually with His guidance. It is one of our greatest assignments. As noted by BBC Bitesize (https://www.bbc.co.uk), a parent's role is to provide a safe, loving environment and support a child's emotional, social, and cognitive development, while making decisions that ensure their overall well-being.

Over time, my family found a sense of peace and balance, which was important to me. With that stability, I refocused on my career. After seven years in my department and experience in the healthcare industry, I felt ready to grow. I had moved from the Atlanta team to the national team in a lateral role as a contract negotiator for ancillary services across various markets, seeking new opportunities.

On the national team, I consistently exceeded expectations, took on additional responsibilities, and documented my work to reflect my contributions. I also earned my master's degree in healthcare administration. Despite my efforts and desire to grow, the support I needed did not fully materialize, something I had not experienced before, as previous managers had always encouraged my development. I valued the review process as a time not only to assess performance but to plan for future growth, so this was disappointing.

Still, I remained diligent and positive, trusting God's timing. As it says in Galatians 6:9, *"Let us not grow weary in doing good..."* and in Proverbs 22:29, diligence leads to greater opportunities. I believed that working faithfully meant serving God through my work and through people.

I was grateful for a previous manager in the Atlanta market who truly invested in my growth. Under his leadership, I developed strong skills in provider contracting, recruiting healthcare providers, managing networks, negotiating cost-saving deals, and building lasting relationships. I worked with a wide range of facilities, including urgent care centers, ambulatory surgery centers, hospitals, radiology centers, and more.

I also became a subject matter expert on the Atlanta team for IVF center contracts, negotiating reimbursements for services that helped women pursue motherhood. That work felt especially meaningful. My career has never just been a job; it's a calling that allows me to make a real difference in people's lives.

CHAPTER

Ten

Holding on to Hope, Faith, and God While Living in the Worst Pain

L ife was peaceful, and I felt like everything was going smoothly in all areas of my life. 2019 was a good year for the most part. We all embraced the new year with happiness and full of affirmations and manifestations that we initiated in the year before. I felt that 2020 was going to be full of happiness at a new level for my family and me. I continued to pour into my children, helping them to decide on the path they would like to take as a career or profession. They both decided to go on a different route than what Mom suggested. My daughter had just recently passed her medical assistant examination after completing the program at Clayton State University, and my son was preparing for barber school the following month to obtain his license to become a barber and to eventually start his own business in that profession.

One evening, my family and I were all preparing for bed. In fact, my son was in his bed, and I was in my room preparing for bed as well. I heard my son's phone ring, and I could hear him talking, and then he walked out the front door. I fell into a deep sleep not long after.

The next morning, I showered and logged in for work. The day was super busy, and I was consumed with a lot to do. As the day wound down, I received a phone call from my daughter around 4 p.m. asking me if my son was home in his bedroom. She told me that one of our neighbor friends had seen a message on the doorbell camera post that there was the body of a Black male near the pavilion in our subdivision. I walked to my son's bedroom, and his door was closed. Of course, I thought that he was asleep because sometimes he would sleep in and start his day a little later if he was up late. When I opened his bedroom and saw that my child was NOT in his bed. I immediately LOST MY MIND!

I tried calling his phone several times, but he did not answer. My son would typically call me back rather quickly when he missed my calls. I called my mom and LS, and I immediately went to the pavilion area. When I made it there, I saw yellow tape around the pavilion area of our subdivision where we lived. The police would not allow anyone near the scene. All I could do was cry and scream because I knew in my heart that something was not right. I ran to the house of the guy who called my son yesterday evening, as he was the last person I heard my son talking to on the phone the evening before. I saw two cars in his driveway and a car parked on the street, in front of their house. I ran to their front door and banged on it loudly and hard. I continued to bang, but no one answered the door. I knew that someone was in that house and avoided answering the door.

I ran back to the scene that was completely surrounded by yellow tape. As an emotional mess, my daughter, close friends, neighbors, and I waited until the police came to us to confirm the identity of the person lying inside the parameters of the yellow tape near the subdivision pavilion. The wait felt like a lifetime. I was shaking and so distraught because I kept calling my son's cell phone with no answer and no call back. I knew something was not right. This was NOT like my baby, he always calls back!

There was one police officer who was on the scene who attended high school with my children and recently joined the police force. My son had just recently congratulated him on joining the police force and on the birth of his new baby. This young man was able to identify my son immediately, and when the lead officer walked over to us, he handed me my son's keys and regretfully informed us that the person who was found deceased near the neighborhood's pavilion was my son, VP Jr.

My daughter and I lost all control! It was as if my body had frozen. It was a complete out-of-body experience that I do not wish on any parent or family member. I could not wrap my heart or mind around what just happened to my child, my firstborn, my only son, my baby boy. I was in total disbelief and in a state of total shock! The pain that I experienced can't be described or explained. I could not believe that someone had taken my child's life. The child that I birthed. The child whom I introduced to God. The child who knew God and would give the shirt off his back to anyone. From that moment, my life would never be the same. From that point, our lives would never be the same. My heart was broken forever. Our hearts were broken forever. I did not know how we would move forward in life without our VP Jr.

The police came to our home that evening to discuss any key information that could relate to the case involving my son. Broken-hearted, my daughter and I provided all the information that we had to assist the authorities in arresting and charging the person who had done this to my son. The police searched my son's bedroom for any clues surrounding our tragedy. My daughter and I shared everything that we had to share and were also vigilant on our end in helping the police in bringing justice to the guilty party and justice for our VP Jr.

My daughter and my son were very close, and so there were a vast number of details surrounding discussions and information that VP Jr. shared with her that catapulted the direction of the case. We knew in our hearts who had done this deplorable act against my son, and we were going to do everything in our power to make sure that he would be held accountable. The detective overseeing our case made our case a priority and assured us that he would work around the clock to solve this case. He was a detective who sacrificed his personal time to work on this case. I thanked God for him being such a diligent and focused detective who worked around the clock to get answers and to hold the guilty accountable.

The police eventually left our home, and a family member reserved a room for us at a local hotel that night because it was very difficult to remain at home that night. I did not sleep at all, and all I could do was look up at the hotel room ceiling, crying. My daughter said the same for herself. This type of pain cuts deep, and this type of pain can only be managed by the hand and solace of God.

Matthew 5:4 says, *"Blessed are those who mourn, for they will be comforted."* We needed God more than anything, and we needed Him right there and at that very moment, as it felt as if life was sucked out of me.

Two days before losing my son, my daughter and I were walking around the neighborhood with my young grandson while he rode his new bike. It was early evening, and my daughter mentioned that she had a strange feeling while we were outside. I told her that I did not, but as we walked closer to my truck, which was parked near the neighborhood pavilion, I felt an uneasiness in my spirit, and I did not understand what was being communicated to me at that time. I am convinced that the Universe speaks to our souls in every situation before and after something transpires in our lives. I am a praying woman, and was a praying mother at that time as well, but going through this horrific experience that has forced me to move forward in life without one of my babies has brought me to another level of closeness to God. All I had was God to comfort me, sustain me, and carry me through. God knew what I needed to keep going. The pain was so deep, and my heart was shattered.

Psalm 23:4 says, *"Even though I walk through the darkest valley, I will fear no evil, for you are with me; your rod and your staff, they comfort me,"* was at that time and continues to be the summary of my walk with God since I lost my son. I knew that my son was with Him.

As family and friends near and far began to flood into town, we had prepared for a balloon release in honor of my son's life and young legacy. As we pulled out photos and talked about our memories and the love that we experienced with VP Jr., it became more emotional. My son was my very first reason to aspire in life, to work hard, and to dare to dream bigger and be greater for myself and for my family. And in the process, Satan's lies and doubt tried to creep in, but God blocked them all and reminded me who I was and whose I was, fearfully and wonderfully made by Him.

My goal was to create a life for my children so that they may be able to thrive and excel in their own endeavors and dreams. Most importantly, for them to walk in who God called them to be and what God called them to do. My son's life was cut short for no reason. I do know that God handles the vengeance, and the guilty party or parties will receive God's wrath in due time. There is no expiration date for vengeance on this type of heinous act against my baby.

As our family and friends gathered, we cried, and we laughed at the beautiful memories that my son left behind. My son was way beyond his years in mind and spirit, and taught me many things in life. He had such great wisdom at a young age, and he inspired me every day as he continued to mature into the young man that he had become. Proverbs 10:1 says, *"A wise son makes a glad father, but a foolish son is a sorrow to his mother."* My son made us all very proud. The balloon release was a success, reflecting my son's life in such a loving and respectful way. There was a very good turnout of love and support from many.

As VP Jr.'s mother, I spoke proudly of my son and how he was a young man of kindness, compassion, integrity, and leadership. VP Jr.'s other loved ones and friends spoke on how much he had a positive impact on their lives and how he made them laugh with the funniest jokes. Many of his peers spoke about how he always encouraged them, motivated them, and inspired them in life. We felt my son's spirit in our presence as we honored him, and I knew that he was well pleased with the outpour of love shown.

That same weekend, my mother and I began planning my son VP Jr.'s funeral in Upstate New York, where his father was laid to rest. It was the hardest thing I have ever faced. How do I move forward without my baby boy, my firstborn, my best friend? Only God carried me through. My heart was shattered, and I felt overwhelmed with grief. We needed Him more than ever.

My mother stood by me, and together, though inconsolable, we made the final arrangements with God's guidance. Just before leaving for New York, the police informed us they had captured the suspect in connection with another incident and were holding him without bail. I immediately thanked God. I knew in my spirit there was a risk he could have fled, but now he was exactly where he needed to be. The investigation continued, and I felt relief knowing he would be held accountable.

My daughter played a crucial role. She stayed in contact with people who had been around her brother, carefully keeping messages and details from their conversations. She shared this information with me and the detectives, which led to a major break in the case. She even connected with a key witness willing to testify. I thank God my children were so close; it made all the difference.

With this update, we traveled to New York with a little more peace as we prepared for VP Jr.'s service. Before facing that day, I prayed and spoke to God, holding onto His Word: *"I lift up my eyes to the mountains… my help comes from the Lord"* (Psalm 121:1-2). I also spent time alone with my son at the funeral home, praying and pouring my heart out to God for strength and peace.

Family and friends came from near and far, New York, Georgia, Syracuse, and New York City. His close friends drove from Georgia, and others flew in. His siblings, godparents, and loved ones all gathered to honor him. Their presence meant so much because my son loved deeply.

We prepared everything in his favorite colors, red, black, and white. The flowers were beautiful, and we met with the pastor and first lady, who prayed over us and offered comfort. They led the service with grace. VP Jr.'s friends spoke so beautifully about him, reminding me of the incredible young man he was and the circle he built around him.

I could feel his presence. In so many ways, it felt like he was with us. Still, the reality was heavy; life without my son would be a long, painful journey. I already missed his laugh, his jokes, his love, the light he brought into our lives.

We will miss him every day until we meet again. My heart is in heaven with my son. Losing my firstborn is a pain we will carry always, taking it one day at a time. Through it all, we continue to lean on God, now more than ever.

CHAPTER

Eleven

Holding onto God's Hand in the Storm

A couple of days after VP Jr.'s funeral service, we flew back to Georgia from New York, and as we were awaiting my neighbor to pick us up from the airport, I received a call from LS and he was encouraging me, out of concern to move from the house into an apartment for a while and that he will help with doing anything needed to make this happen. I was on the same page as him because we did not need to be, nor did we want to be, in such an upsetting and traumatic environment where we currently lived. In addition to that, we needed to be assured that we were living in a safe environment.

Immediately, I started to decide on an area where we would be most comfortable. I chose an area where I loved to go to shop, get massages, facials, and dine on some weekends or when I had some downtime, my area where I went for peace. I thought of Peachtree City (PTC), which was a little further south of town off Interstate 85. It was a great location to live until I was able to sell my current home. It was an area where many of the airline professionals lived before and after retirement. The area is very quiet, peaceful, and family-oriented.

My daughter and I immediately began the apartment search, and after about a week or two, we were able to narrow down to one in the PTC area and began the moving process. At the same time, I met with a realtor and began getting my home prepared to be placed on the market to sell. We started packing and had some of the bigger appliances placed in storage. It was an emotional and busy time for us. My son's birthday was three weeks after his passing, so in deep sadness, we honored him for his birthday that he was so anxiously awaiting and preparing to celebrate prior to everything that happened.

A group of us, family and friends, decided to gather at one of the national golfing entertainment venues in the Atlanta area, Top Golf, to celebrate my baby boy. As sad as we were, we were able to muster up some smiles and pictures as we celebrated VP Jr., and in remembering my son for the kind, loving, and funny young man that he was. At his young age, my son had already established a legacy built on trendsetting, leadership, and love. My son displayed the character of a young lightworker, and so I was a very proud mother. I learned so much more about my son from the wonderful words his peers spoke of him and how much he encouraged and showed compassion and respect for them. I could not ask God for a better child.

In this trying hour, God was my safe space. I leaned on Him and cried out to Him at any time, day or night. I would lie on the bedroom floor in the apartment before the movers delivered our furniture, and I cried every night until I fell asleep, missing my son terribly, feeling helpless. Every night, I literally felt God's hands on me, cradling me to sleep. This time in my life was one of total and complete isolation, not because it just so happened to be a nationwide shutdown due to the COVID pandemic that just overtook the world, but the isolation that I needed to allow God to pour into me each day as I grieved, to strengthen me while I was weak. He was building something up in me as I prayed.

At that most critical time in our lives, God was very much near us, and He showed us this in some way or form each day. This gave us comfort and peace that surpassed all understanding. The isolation period of the COVID pandemic also gave us the stillness we needed to allow God to carry us. All we knew was pain. So God kept His hands on us.

Romans 5:3-5 reads, *"Not only that, but we rejoice in our sufferings, knowing that suffering produces endurance, and endurance produces character, and character produces hope, and hope does not put us to shame, because God's love has been poured into our hearts through the Holy Spirit who has been given to us."* It took the hand of God to give me the strength to move forward with endurance and hope. God continued to hold my hand and continued to send the right people and opportunities to help me navigate all that was on my plate, in addition to being able to grieve. I still had to focus on my daughter and grandson, helping them through their grieving, their needs, and our transition into a brand-new routine and life without my son. We were desperately missing him.

I drew closer to God as He drew closer to me. According to James 4:8, it states to *"Draw near to God, and He will draw near to you."* Also, Psalm 73:28 (NIV) iterates, *"But as for me, it is good to be near God. I have made the Sovereign Lord my refuge; I will tell of all your deeds."* A daily encounter with God builds up in us a strength, hope, and faith that will break down any barrier of doubt, confusion, and weariness.

In the highest form of devastation, if we draw close to God, He will meet us where we are, and He will give us what we need to push through and to finish the race of life. My family and I were wrapped in the loving arms and care of God amid insurmountable pain. We prayed for peace, and He provided us with peace. He kept us, and we continued to hold on to Him. As we held on to God's hand, He guided and protected us.

After we returned to Georgia from my baby VP Jr.'s service, a close friend in New York sent me Psalm 30:5: *"Weeping may endure for a night, but joy comes in the morning."* That verse stayed with me. Along with daily devotionals from my cousin, it gave me hope, peace, and the strength to keep going, even in the hardest part of my journey.

Choosing to keep going helped me walk in purpose. I became committed to advocating for gun violence and mental health awareness. In honor of my son's legacy, I decided to start a nonprofit that will offer two scholarships each year, the Voiese Pinn Jr. Annual Scholarship, for student entrepreneurs and leaders in the Henry County school district. VP Jr. made us so proud as a young scholar and business owner.

As we searched for balance, we stayed connected virtually with pastors, family, friends, and work. Since I already worked from home, that remained steady. We celebrated birthdays and holidays online, which helped keep us emotionally and spiritually grounded. During COVID, the isolation also gave us time to slow down, focus on God, and care for ourselves. We took nature walks, rested, and allowed God to restore us.

There were moments I felt my son's presence. One night, not long after his passing, I woke up around 1 a.m. crying. The bathroom light blinked three times, and in my heart, I knew it was him reminding me he loved me. I needed that.

LS was with me every step of the way, and I am deeply grateful for his presence in my life. Through everything, I remained focused on peace, self-care, and grieving in a healthy way, making sure my children did the same.

After four months in our apartment in PTC, ongoing issues and an unresponsive landlord led us to break the lease and move back home in July 2020. But being there didn't bring peace; it was a constant reminder of the worst day of our lives.

Less than a year later, I received a cash offer from an investor to buy the house. After confirming it was legitimate, I accepted. I began searching for a new home and found a builder whose design I loved. The buyer allowed us to stay in the already-sold house until construction was complete, which was a blessing. Within four to five months, we moved into our new home. It was a fresh start, one we truly needed. God's timing was perfect.

Around that time, I had also started my master's in healthcare administration in October 2020, balancing work by day and school at night and on weekends. It was demanding but worth it.

That holiday season brought unexpected joy; my daughter shared that she was expecting a baby girl. In the midst of everything, it was a beautiful reminder of life, hope, and new beginnings.

LS and I continued to share updates and milestones in our lives whenever we found the opportunity to do so. I was so sad to hear about the passing of his mother. It broke my heart as I knew how close he and his siblings were to his mother. He and I had previously talked when she was ill, and he asked if I would pray for her, and, of course, I did. We both shared that our daughters were expecting baby girls, and I was also able to share the good news about the closing of the new house, and he was very happy to hear the wonderful news.

We talked in February 2022, and I was excited to tell him that I would be done with my degree in May 2022, three months away. He mentioned that maybe I should go for my PhD for an additional two years because by then he will be retired. I told him that two additional years of school would wear me out completely because I had gotten so exhausted from writing so many research papers in the master's program.

A few weeks later, in March 2022, LS texted and invited me to brunch. I agreed. When I saw him, he seemed stressed, unlike his usual self, but we still caught up, sharing family updates and photos like we always did. Afterward, as he walked me to my car, I asked if he had a girlfriend, since it had been a while since we'd seen each other. He didn't answer; he simply kissed me and left.

My daughter and his niece stayed close, so they kept in touch. In July 2022, my daughter told me LS had recently gotten engaged. I was shocked. I called him and told him that if it was true, he should not contact me again. That was our final conversation. I deleted his number and moved forward. It hurt deeply, especially because we had often talked about a future together.

Soon after, a woman I had never met, his fiancée, began targeting me on social media. Ironically, I had only joined Facebook in 2021 to support my work as a new author in *"Stand Up! Resilient Black Women Who Are Shaping the World With Their Faith, Volume One."* A book that inspired me to continue with my passion to write as a solo author. (A copy of this book is available on my website, https://www.changinglanesenterprizellc.com/). The testimonies in this book are powerful and encourage strong faith in action. That platform, meant for a purpose, became a place of attack.

What followed was nearly four years of online harassment, lies, insults, slander, and mockery across Facebook, Instagram, and LinkedIn. Others, many who didn't know me, joined in. Even some public figures spoke on things they knew nothing about. Though I was often blocked from seeing posts directly, I could feel the weight of the negativity. Still, I held onto God. I trusted His promise to fight for me and never leave me. Despite the attacks, I chose obedience. I drew closer to Him and continued to grow into who He called me to be, a woman who walks in truth, humility, confidence, and dignity. As a mother and now a grandmother, I remain mindful of the example I set.

There were also those who supported and encouraged me, and I'm grateful for them. Through it all, I stayed focused on God, protecting my peace and nurturing a healthy environment for my family. *"Be still and know that I am God"* carried me through. I believed His promise to contend with those who contend with me.

As difficult as it was, I chose to forgive. I refused to let others' actions weigh me down. Forgiveness allowed me to walk in freedom and remain open to God's blessings. There is no greater peace than moving forward in His transformation and guidance.

I continue to trust God in all things. Every challenge became a stepping stone, strengthening my faith and resilience. As I *"change lanes"* in life, I trust that He is guiding me, leading me toward purpose, favor, and the blessings ahead.

The trial for the case involving my son had been delayed until early 2023 due to the impact of the COVID epidemic. We were nervous yet ready to get the difficult process done with, and justice served. The key witness and many other witnesses involved in the case, including my daughter and me, were given a subpoena to be cross-examined at the trial.

I was so thankful that the key witness was able to make it to the stand and testify, which was the leading evidence needed to move the direction of the trial where we needed it to go.

The detective who oversaw our case, along with the state prosecutor that my family is so grateful for, was able to close out the trial with a GUILTY verdict outcome and served the guilty party, life without the possibility of parole, plus an additional 15 years. This person took my son's life for no reason.

My family's life will never be the same. My son will never have the opportunity to marry and have a family of his own because of this horrible person and the horrible act that stole his life. So after hearing the verdict, we thanked God for justice. My final statement toward the guilty party and his family was, *"God will claim vengeance on all of you!"* My God made sure that vengeance was served! Justice was served in a mighty way. God has shown me time and time again that He never fails nor has He ever lost a battle.

Choosing to change lanes and to be obedient to God in all that He has for us will provide us with a life that is intentional, purposeful, and impactful. When choosing God as our CEO, we will never go under or bankrupt in our spirit. We will never have to worry or stress about the future forecast of our lives, and we shall definitely trust that the return on our faith investments will bring about endless peace and prosperity from God, our Father.

CHAPTER

Twelve

Leveraging GODpportunities and Transformational Testimonials to Encourage

I coined *"GODportunities"* as opportunities from God that are placed directly on our paths. I am sharing mine for the purpose of testimonial encouragement.

I have always had an interest in obtaining an advanced degree, but I held off because I was still repaying undergraduate student loans. I was not interested in adding to the pot by accumulating more student loan debt. As I developed in my role at work, I eventually decided to enroll in a master's program at the University of Arizona to obtain my master's degree in healthcare administration. The timing was perfect for me as my employer at the time was offering a shared savings education package where the school and my employer paid the bulk of the tuition, and my contribution was a small portion of the whole. God's timing is always perfect!

Ecclesiastes 3:11 says, *"Yet God has made everything beautiful for its own time. He has planted eternity in the human heart, but even so, people cannot see the whole scope of God's work from beginning to end."* This opportunity was full of God's goodness! God aligned me with a chance to access my advanced degree with minimal out-of-pocket costs and zero loans. I am grateful for God's hand over this chance to advance in my education and knowledge in the industry that I enjoyed serving in. The following year, God extended His kindness to me again. Under the Biden administration, I was relieved from paying back a hefty balance in student loans that I had been paying for over ten years. God worked it out in my favor. I paid my dues in the student loan world, so *"Bye now, it has been stressful knowing you."*

Receiving the paid-in-full student loan email from the Biden Administration was a very pleasant surprise and a blessing at the same time. I continued to work diligently in my role, remaining open to growth and new opportunities. By 2024, I had reached my 17th year at the health insurance company and over 20 years in the healthcare industry. Work-life balance became essential to me, as I valued self-care and family time just as much as my professional commitments.

In late 2024, I was impacted by a company-wide layoff from the

Fortune 500 health insurance company where I had worked for almost 20 years. I remained calm, recognizing that if God allowed it, He was redirecting my steps toward something better. He had already nudged me that it was time to move forward.

After the layoff, I felt called to establish my own managed care consulting business, Changing Lanes Enterprise LLC, offering managed care contract negotiation, contracting workshops and training, business coaching, credentialing services, and consulting. This path toward entrepreneurship, something I had never envisioned as my primary source of income, aligned with God's plan for my financial freedom.

To support this transition, I hired a professional coach who helped me gain clarity and recognize how my existing skills could serve as the foundation for this new chapter. God also used a friend to confirm another calling: writing my book, *"Changing Lanes with God as my CEO: Finding Purpose and Prosperity Through Divine Direction."* She shared this message with me directly, and I chose to walk in obedience.

Throughout our journeys, God connects us with like-minded professionals and places us in environments where we can grow, build, and even serve as change agents. Sometimes, He transitions us into roles or spaces that better align with our next phase.

At the time of the layoff, I felt no fear, only understanding. God had already revealed that my time at the company had ended. I had even prayed that if I needed to leave, it would happen through a layoff, and it did. Despite the uncertainty, I trusted that His plan was greater because He sees what lies ahead.

This mindset is essential when God calls us to shift or change lanes. I remember hearing Him say, *"Trust Me,"* one evening at Woman Evolve in Dallas, Texas, in 2024. That same trust applies to both our professional and personal lives.

One of my biggest leaps of faith was relocating from New York to Georgia with my two young children, leaving behind our familiar environment and support system. Once I accepted that God was orchestrating my steps for a career promotion, everything else fell into place successfully.

When the Lord breathes on our goals, manifestations, and affirmations, success follows.

Experiencing a lay-off or any disappointment can leave us with a lot of questions and frustration; however, if we look to God and seek His will and His way for us, we shall find out what it is that He is doing for us or through us in this process and in this season. We should choose to understand the new change that He is incorporating in our lives.

There is always something good that comes from change when we are seeking God to guide and direct us. We do not have to view change as a loss. Change is bound to happen. So, it really helps us to think and move strategically in situations such as this. With this, we will know what steps to take next on our journey.

Matthew 6:33 says, *"But seek first His Kingdom and His righteousness, and all things will be added to you."* This not only applies to our jobs and careers, but it also applies to everything in life. So, when there is confusion and chaos around us, we must be still, calm, and trust that God will direct our paths and, most importantly, He will always provide and guide us. We just need to be alert, aware, and willing. Regularly reading our Bible will allow God to feed us what He wants us to receive in that moment so that we may prepare for what He wants us to do next. The process can feel nerve-wracking and even a bit scary when sudden, life-changing moments and *"changing lanes"* opportunities arise.

Not knowing what is next in our career or financial journey can make us a little weary and nervous, but I can say that I have been placed in a position where my only hope and strength came simply from trusting God's direction and guidance, not my own and certainly not man's. When money in my bank account did not add up to my monthly expenses, but trusting in God was the bank deposit that I needed.

This past year's (2025) job market had fallen below expectations and was the weakest since the pandemic, going from two million jobs created in 2024 to only 584,000 in 2025, per the US Bureau of Labor Statistics. The most powerful business move we can make in today's job market is to yield to God and what He has directed us to do next. He is the Boss, He is the CEO, He is the Financial Advisor, and the Peace and Wellness Restorer. Talk to Him, and He will respond. Be alert and aware of His response when He delivers it to you. He has the *"playbook"* of what moves we must make on the playing field of life. He already knows what the financial forecast will be and the impact it will have on our future finances and endeavors.

At times, when we think it is the end of the world because of a *"loss"* or *"setback"* that stems from a layoff or any form of loss, it is really a way of protection or preparation for something better than what we hoped or prayed for. When we wait on God, we must do it with anticipation, focusing on what God wants us to embrace in that hour, to leave behind what is not supposed to go with us, or to simply embrace the process or journey that He wants us to learn and walk in. Claim abundance and success. Claim growth. Claim increase. Claim stability. Claim healing.

I've come to understand that nothing is wasted with God. Everything He uses to shape us prepares us for who we are called to be and where we are going next. He can even restore what was lost with an increase often better than before or beyond what we expected.

But we won't recognize His direction without consistent communication. We must stay open to how He speaks through prayer, reading the Bible, journaling, and sometimes through others, like a pastor or spiritually connected person. Fasting can also help us focus and hear Him more clearly.

During the time I was out of work, I was able to assist my daughter with my four grandchildren (Josiah, Jolani, Jurzi, and Jireh) in many ways, and this is what she needed during that specific time with a busy and hectic work schedule. My situation gave me freedom to help loved ones and others by filling in the gap where I was needed, and this is a form of ministry.

Supporting others and volunteering our free time in helping or serving others is also a form of ministry that is fulfilling and, most importantly, pleasing to God. When our time permits, let's share it with others.

Sometimes, God wants to use us for humanitarian work for a period instead of corporate work. His paycheck is much better. His return is greater, and His dividends outweigh all the others in the stock market.

Timing is everything, and God aligns all things according to His designated time. When we feel the urge to rush or delay, we must recognize that trying to control it will not work. Everything unfolds within His timing, often to prepare us for something important. Sometimes, opportunities come within small windows, so we must stay ready.

Networking is powerful. Many business professionals I've met at events have connected me to valuable individuals and GODpportunities that supported my growth, business, and exposure.

Building and maintaining contact lists is essential for communication and marketing. Whenever I attend events, I add business card details to my directory. There are also many free workshops and training available locally and online for various skills.

Platforms like Eventbrite help you find workshops, webinars, and networking events, many with free registration. You can also explore courses and certifications through Coursera, ed2go, and Xero. Joining social media or local groups aligned with your business, attending networking events, choosing a mentor, and trying free business platforms can all move you forward.

Always remember, *"Changing lanes"* may be the blessing on the other side of being stuck in bumper-to-bumper traffic.

About the Author

Tawisha Nikki Buckingham is a woman of faith who prioritizes God and her family. She is the mother of VP Jr. and VV, and a grandmother to four grandchildren: Josiah, Jolani, Jurzi, and Jireh.

She holds a Master's in Healthcare Administration from the University of Arizona Global Campus and a Bachelor's in Political Science from SUNY Buffalo. Born and raised in Upstate New York, Tawisha has lived in Georgia for the past 20 years.

Tawisha enjoys southern cuisine, seafood, and a good salad. She loves traveling, the beach, and nature walks, which bring her peace, and she strives to carry love and light wherever she goes.